Ink

JADE HERNÁNDEZ

This book is a work of fiction. Any reference to historical events, people or places are used fictitiously. Other names, characters, places and events are products of the author's imagination, and any resemblance to actual events or places or persons, living or dead, is entirely coincidental.

Copyright © 2023 by Jade Hernández

All rights reserved, including the right of reproduction in whole or in part in any form. No part of this book may be reproduced or transmitted in any form or by any means, electronic or mechanical, including photocopying, recording, or by any information storage and retrieval system, without written permission from the author.

Softcover Cover design and typography image by: Temptation Creations

Edited by: Lisa Nieves

Content Warning

INK IS A SEMI-DARK Motorcycle Club romance story and contains scenes that may be triggering to some readers. This short story contains depictions of gang violence, mentions of cartels, violence, strict/abusive mother, gore, guns, drugs, alcohol consumption, slut shaming, misogyny, machismo, kidnapping, the spoken threat of sexual assault (though none occurs), the mention of sexual harrassment in the FMC's past, tattoos, and death. If such material offends you, please do not pick up this book or approach it with caution. Also, if the word *gringo* offends you, maybe don't pick this up as it is used liberally.

This book also contains consensual sexual themes and kinks, such as boss/employee relationships, sexual tension, choking, rough sex, tattoo sex play, slapping, and spanking.

Author's Note

INK IS A CONTEMPORARY Motorcycle Club romance story that takes place in Mexico and features gang violence, motorcycles, and cholas & cholos. The content within this story is purely fictional and is not meant to depict any real world events, does not reflect on a singular group of people, and is not meant to stereotype. This is my fictional, loose interpretation as a Mexican author who currently lives and has lived in Mexico for a majority of my life and who has put in a lot of time of extensive research on the characters. That being said, if anything within this story offends anyone, that is not my intent and I deeply apologize. If anything inside offends you, and you wish to let me know, please do not hesitate to contact me, as I am not perfect and always aim to do better and be a better person.

About the Author

Jade Hernández is a proud Mexican-American woman who strives to bring more Latinx stories to life within the contemporary romance genre. You may know her as Aleera Anaya Ceres, the USA Today Bestselling Author of diverse fantasy and paranormal works. Under this new penname, she aims to represent her culture by writing sweet, dark, gritty, and fun stories for all. As an introvert, Jade prefers to stay inside with a good book, collect tarot cards, and she's recently found a love for book boxes! She currently lives in Tlaxcala, Mexico with her husband and children.

OTHER WORKS BY JADE HERNÁNDEZ

El Rancho Los Corazones series
Learn to Love You
Los Diablos Motorcycle Club
Ink
Miguel

Feminine Rage

For the women with rage inside them.
Let it fester.
Become the villain you were meant to be.

Motorcycle Club Lingo

Road name - Nicknames given to members of the club.

Cut/Cuero - Leather jacket vests with their club name, Road name, and designation.

Brothers/Hermanos - Club members.

Prospects - Trainees. They are not pledged members of the club. They do the grunt work and go through hazing to prove themselves and their loyalty to the club.

Puta/Putas - Club whores/club girls who entertain and sleep with the club members in exchange for housing, protection, or jobs.

Misa/Church - Club meetings.

Old Lady/Vieja - Equivalent to wife.

Los Diablos Members and Roles

HERE IS A GUIDE to the members of Los Diablos MC, their real names, positions, and their Old Ladies (Viejas) if they have them.

Loco

Adrián Ramos, the **President** of Los Diablos. He is the leader, and while the MC is a brotherhood that votes on certain issues, the President is ultimately the one who makes final decisions.

Miguel

Miguel Salvador Lopez, **Vice President** of Los Diablos. He is the President's right hand man. If, in the event that the President is unavailable to perform his duties for any reason, the VP takes over as leader of the club in his absence.

Mayan

Tanok Ortega Coatl, **Secretary** of Los Diablos. The secretary is in charge of keeping reports and paperwork for the club, whether that be for illegal activities or voting, note-taking, etc within the MC.

Cubano

Juan Diego Luna, **Treasurer** of Los Diablos. The treasurer is in charge of the money. He handles business expenses, payments, etc that involve any club activity.

JADE HERNÁNDEZ

Chema
José Maria Iglesias, **Sergeant at Arms** of Los Diablos. The *Sgt at Arms* is in charge of security within the club. It is his job to make sure all members are safe and following the rules of the MC. He is also in charge of ensuring security within and outside of the club and is required to report any oncoming or suspected threats to the council.

Crank
Luis Carlos Gonzalez, **Road Captain** of Los Diablos. The Road Captain is in charge of plotting routes and runs for the club. Whenever they ride out, he will be in charge of formations and the journey as well as the vehicles they take when they go.

Ángel
Jose Ángel Paredes, **Enforcer** of Los Diablos. The Enforcer is similar to the Sgt at Arms. They are in charge of making sure members are following the rules and they dish out punishment within and outside of the club to those who don't. They're a club protector.

Ink
Benito Juárez Sánchez, member of Los Diablos, though not part of the council. Xiomara Nava is his Viejita.

BLURB

XIOMARA

My whole life has been riddled with nothing but bad luck, especially when it comes to jobs.

I can never seem to hold anything down, and the truth is, nobody wants to work with someone as volatile and angry as me.

But to take care of my family, I need money, and when the opportunity arises to work the front desk at Devil's Ink, the local Motorcycle Club's tattoo shop, I'll do everything I can to not mess this up. It doesn't matter that there are rumors of darkness and blood surrounding Los Diablos MC. Or that my dangerous new boss doesn't think I can do the job. Or that his hungry eyes follow me every step of the way, inciting a lust for someone I can never be with, someone who hates everything about me.

I guess if there's one thing they're about to find out, it's that violence never scared me anyway.

Ink

Only the best work at Devil's Ink and Xiomara is anything but. With a reputation like hers, I knew she was sure to fail within the week.

JADE HERNÁNDEZ

I never expected that her steely determination to prove me wrong would result in a lust I don't need or want. I'm her boss. She's my employee. Anything between us is bound to end in disaster.

That doesn't stop my gaze from going over her body. Or obsessing over her laughter. Or wanting my ink tattooed on her skin.

I try to tell myself that my lifestyle is too dangerous for someone like her. And when the violence and blood of my MC touches her perfect skin, I know I'll do anything to protect her from it.

I guess she'll see for herself how many souls a Diablo can reap for his woman.

Chapter One
Xiomara

I curved my nails into the battered leather of my piece of shit steering wheel, sitting inside my piece of shit car, with *Molotov* on full blast as I tried to muster the courage to get out and go inside.

The sign outside of the building was nondescript, simple, and mocking. *Devil's Ink*. Appropriately named, I supposed, with the horned skull spray painted on the outer wall by a talented hand, not to mention the fact that this tattoo parlor belonged to Los Diablos MC.

They were a local, one-percenter motorcycle club, and that's really all I knew about them.

I probably should've worked harder to find out more. But crime always ran rampant in Mexico, and it was too hard to keep track of all the shady shit that went down. Prostitution, drugs, guns... It was all the same at that point. No one in our little state of Tlaxcala was free from a life of debauchery. Not me. Especially not the MC.

Still, a part of me wondered if I should have been smarter about this. Some organizations were very machista in their beliefs, and women were rarely safe from the wrath of misogynistic men. If they weren't careful, they'd find themselves turning tricks on the side of highways late into the night for cartels, only to crawl back to their jailors out of pure fear or addiction, if not both.

Los Diablos wasn't a cartel, but I was sure they could be just as brutal.

And I had to be careful, considering I was going to be working for them starting today.

You know, if I ever found the courage to actually *go in* and start.

Disengaging my trembling fingers from the wheel, I yanked my headphones out, the string snagging against the length of my shiny black hair. After struggling with the wire, I tossed it onto the passenger seat and grabbed my phone. My thumbs flew across the screen as I logged into one of my favorite online communities.

I told myself I just needed a little encouragement as I typed up a message and pressed send, biting on my plump bottom lip as I waited.

An influx of responses came in almost immediately. An array of 'Good luck!' 'Tú puedes!' 'You got this!'

Simple messages from an online support group for Latine people, but they filled me with exactly what I needed to finally pocket my phone into my belted black pants and hop out of the car.

Up close, the details of the painted diablo logo were clearer. It'd obviously been there for a while, the edges chipping, cement cracking and missing in patches.

I wanted to shudder at the thought of what the inside looked like, but I held myself back. I was in no way prissy and had dealt with my hand of shitty jobs before. This should have been no different.

Only... I was fired from my last job at the gas station when I kneed my manager in the nuts for copping a feel behind the cash register. I did more to him than just kick him in his precious balls, but I didn't like to think about that. If I did, all I'd see was the disappointment in my mamá's eyes as I told her I lost yet another job. The memory was a punch to the gut.

I was lucky enough a distant cousin hooked me up at this place. Said she knew the owners or some shit.

I couldn't afford to fuck up this time. My family was counting on me to bring money in for gas and food.

That meant I couldn't be fucking late.

Taking a breath, I steeled my spine and pushed through the front doors of Devil's Ink. Immediately, I was hit with the scent of tinta. It perfumed through the air; cloying, heady, familiar. Buzzing echoed across the art-clad walls, the vibration pressing down to my bones, comforting and soothing.

If the outside looked shabby, the inside was a work of art. A collage of tattoos on bodies, of instruments and leather. Done up in dark tones of black, burgundy, and warm gray, the waiting area gave off a chill vibe, which was great for anyone nervous about coming in to get tatted up.

I did a slow twirl, taking in the space. So far, I liked what I saw. In the front, there was a long desk with a computer and several stacks of papers. Behind the desk there was a woman with long, dyed purple hair, gauges, and several facial piercings. Behind her, there was the wall that separated the inking area, lit beyond by bright lights and echoing with the steady sound of a tattoo gun.

JADE HERNÁNDEZ

"Can I help you?" the chick asked, taking me in.

I tensed, knowing what she'd see and wondering if she'd judge me for it the way so many others did. For the pants and baggy clothes. For the silver hoops that snagged against curly hair, the penciled in lips, dark brows, and painted mouth.

I knew I looked good, but having her stare at me made me want to fidget where I stood.

I hated being stared at. It made me uncomfortable before it pissed me off, and when my rage-o-meter flew past the limit, I became a different person.

One I wanted to forget.

One that had caused me to lose too many jobs already.

I walked over to the desk, squaring my shoulders. I refused to cow down to her judgmental bullshit, so I met her glare for glare, raising a dark, penciled brow.

"I'm Xiomara. I start work here today."

"Ah. The new secretary." She gave a firm nod and a small hint of a smile broke out on her lips. It changed her fearsome, pierced expression and almost made her pretty. "Good thing you're here. I'm tired of doing this bullshit. It's below my pay grade."

"You tattoo?"

"I do." She beamed with pride then lifted her arms onto the surface of the desk, showing off the array of tattoos that decorated her skin. Everything from roses, to skulls, to naked women.

"Nice," I complimented.

She nodded at the tattoo visible on my arm. Nowhere near as extensive as hers, but the Virgen De Guadalupe on my skin was the only one I allowed myself because of my mamá and her aversion.

When I'd gone home with this one, all brave and bold against my body, she'd slapped the freshly painted art in anger and had gone to pray over my soul.

The experience had left me scared to get a new one. That had been a few years ago, and if I was honest, the urge had never really diminished. Maybe she'd feel differently now than she had then.

Or maybe she'd take a belt to me this time.

Anyway, tattoos were expensive as fuck in this economy, so getting one was out of the question right now considering I was a broke bitch.

"That all you got?"

"For now."

Her hands slapped on the desk. "Stick around; we'll get you filled up in no time."

I could only hope.

"Fer, stop being chismosa with the clients and get your ass to work!" a voice called out from the back area. The deep, husky sound curled through my stomach and dragged my attention up.

A man appeared then, a glare on his face aimed in the woman's–Fer's–direction, right before he snapped it my way.

My breath caught at the piercing, gray gaze that held me captive. A strong, angry expression settled over startling features. The man wasn't attractive. Not really. Not by societal standards, anyway. His nose was just a bit too big and crooked, his stubbled jaw just a bit too squared, lips too full. If the angry, stern face didn't make him attractive in the eyes of society, then the tattoos certainly didn't either.

They covered him up to his neck, sliding and twining over every inch of visible skin. On his arms, his collarbone, disappearing into the material of his tight t-shirt and leather cut.

There was something about his overall vibe, though, that did it for me.

Dangerous had always been my type.

Buenos para nada, my mamá called them.

And fuck, if he wasn't just the type of bad, no-good that could make a good girl worship the horned devil that lived on the front of his leather vest.

Los Diablos MC.

Ink.

"I don't take walk-ins," he said, snapping me out of my stupor. His glare was piercing, cutting, and a total turn-on.

"Not a walk-in, Ink," Fer said, a hint of amusement in her voice. "This is our new secretary."

He assessed me all over again, the slow perusal of his gaze over my body nearly making me shiver. When his rare, gray eyes finally flicked back up to me, he wore an expression of disinterest.

"Hm," he grunted. "Beatriz's cousin?"

"Xiomara," I supplied.

He ignored me and turned to Fer. "Show her the ropes. I want her to be trained by the end of the day." Then he turned back to me. "You get one chance. I was told you fuck up every job you have, so I'm only taking you on as a favor to your cousin. Fuck up *here* and you're out on your fucking ass, got that?" He whipped around and stalked back towards the tattooing area.

Once he was gone, Fer turned to me. "That went well."

That went well? Was she fucking joking?

The man obviously hated me with a single glance. I didn't do well with judgment. It made my heart beat and my palms sweat. It made the rage inside me swell to the surface.

I fought to tamp it down. Lock it up behind a wall of steel.

"Let's get you trained up so the boss man doesn't have a heart attack, yeah? Everything around here is pretty simple. You welcome clients, turn away walk-ins, make appointments on the computer. Know how to work calendars and excel sheets?"

And just like that, she showed me how to manage shit around Devil's Ink.

As far as first days went, this had been one of my best. Things were pretty slow, though, so that could have been why.

I'd been left alone at the front desk while Fer and Ink stayed behind the wall, the steady stream of the tattoo gun buzzing as clients came and went.

When lunch time came, only Fer emerged from the back, a strappy black purse thrown over her shoulder.

"Let's go eat," she ordered. "Ink will man the store. He doesn't have any clients until later."

I agreed, casting a wary glance to the back before I followed her out.

We didn't go very far to eat. Among the bustling fray of the dilapidated street and surrounding locales–*stores*–we flagged down a man on a bike selling tacos de canasta. Attached to the back was a big woven basket lined with blue plastic and cloth. On either side large mayo jars of green and red salsa.

The tacos were tiny, and I got two mixed orders filled with potatoes, tinga, and chicharrón. We ordered a soda from a nearby store and walked over to a bench by the park to eat.

We enjoyed our lunch in silence for a few minutes before Fer leaned back, eyeing me curiously.

"So, what's your deal?" she asked.

I swallowed a sip of soda. "What do you mean?"

She waved in my general direction. "You show up out of the blue and Ink hires you on the spot because of your cousin. Word on the street is you're a fuck up. That true?"

She asked in a curious type of way, and maybe my initial thoughts of her being judgmental were untrue, because she only sounded intrigued and not mean in her inquiry. Still, the question didn't stop me from picking my napkin to little pieces in anxiety.

I didn't do well under scrutiny.

"I mean... kinda?"

"There's a story in there somewhere, mija."

I snort-laughed and put my plate down on the side of the bench.

"There is," I agreed. "But none of them are pleasant. I just can't seem to hold down a job. If that makes me a fuck up, then I guess I am."

"Hmm, that's a nonanswer, but I'll allow it. A bit of advice, though? From a friend?"

A friend? The concept was almost as foreign to me as a stable job. The only friends I knew were those from my online community. People far away and aloof, who could listen to me vent, who only knew me as my username, and who were mysterious and far enough away to not require any commitment.

The concept of someone who I could lean on now was pleasant.

"Yeah?"

"This is a good job. Ink is a huge asshole, and he doesn't give second chances. So don't fuck this one up, okay?"

I sighed and reached for my drink. "Okay."

Except in life there were never any guarantees.

And I'd said I wouldn't fuck mine up any longer.

Yet somehow, I always managed to do it.

Every single time.

Chapter Two
Ink

If I wasn't with my brothers at the Los Diablos clubhouse, then I was drowning myself in work.

I should have taken an hour to go grab a meal with Fer like I usually did. But with her immediately taking the new girl under her wing, I didn't want to encroach on their girl time or whatever the fuck bitches called that shit nowadays.

Besides, I had designs to draft up for some of my more finicky clients. I didn't have time to hang with them, and I had even less desire to get to know the new chick.

She wouldn't last the fucking week anyway, of that I was positive.

Beatriz was an old friend of the club, and when she asked if I could give her cousin a job, I would be remiss to say no. We owed her, and I needed a secretary. With a rise in our clientele, I needed Fer piercing in the back, not dealing with shit in the front.

But after asking Beatriz about her cousin, I'd regretted saying yes without inquiring first. It sounded like she was irresponsible and couldn't hold a job if her life depended on it. That didn't bode well, and I didn't have the time or patience to deal with someone's bullshit. So at the first sign of trouble, I'd fire her ass with no remorse.

Beatriz be damned.

The pencil scratched across the piece of paper, crisscrossing in different degrees of pressure until I'd finally formed an eye.

The piece I was working on was a naked body. My client wanted to immortalize his girl on his skin and was willing to pay a pretty penny for it.

Which meant I had to work overtime to deliver something spectacular. Devil's Ink had a reputation to uphold, after all.

I expected perfection from everyone who worked with me, which made me even more wary of the new girl.

I let my mind go zen as I worked on my project. I didn't stop until the door of the shop chimed and Fer's voice filtered in. I set my pencil to the side, feeling a small cramp work its way through my fingers. I shook it off and stood up, moving to the front.

My eyes strayed to the new girl almost immediately, narrowing on every inch of her. Everything about her spelled trouble. The little chola's big, doe eyes weren't fooling me at all. They were innocent, almost overly so. I didn't trust anyone like that.

It was the Diablo in me.

Our club was involved in guns, sometimes drugs if Loco–the club prez–wanted us to get the extra cash. We lived through dangerous situations every day. It made us wary of everyone and everything.

Especially a pretty face.

She chewed on her plump bottom lip, fighting back a smile as Fer went on about some story or other. I barely heard Fer's words, focused on inhaling every reaction, every expression the new girl made.

Finally, her body tensed like prey catching onto the hint of a predator. Slowly, that dark gaze slid up to me and widened.

She stared at me like I was a fucking ogre, and I couldn't say why that pissed me off more than it probably should have.

"Stop fucking gossiping and get back to work," I snapped.

She jerked back as if I'd slapped her, and her surprised expression morphed into a more serious, almost cold one.

"Yes, sir," she replied and hurried back around the desk to fiddle with the mouse of the computer.

I watched for a minute longer as she stiffly logged info into the spreadsheet before I turned and went back to my work space.

I sensed Fer following me.

I knew what was coming, so it came as no surprise that her fist punched out at my arm in passing.

I sighed.

"Eres un pendejo," she admonished in a whisper, tossing her purse down in her area.

"I'm also your boss," I reminded her sternly.

I didn't need to look at her to know she was rolling her eyes.

"Please," she scoffed. "You won't fire me."

She was right.

She was also the exception.

I'd known Fer for years, and she had gone above and beyond proving her loyalty to me and the club. She worked her ass off here at Devil's Ink and had quickly become family. A person the MC would ride and die for.

In private, she could joke like this.

In public, she knew better.

"She's a nice girl," Fer continued as she washed her hands in a far sink and grabbed sanitary spray to clean her area.

JADE HERNÁNDEZ

"You had one lunch with her."

She winked. "One lunch is all I need to gauge if someone's buena gente or not. Trust me, she's a good one."

"There are a lot of good ones," I scoffed.

But good didn't mean jack shit in our world and this woman, Xiomara Nava, didn't belong in it at all.

Chapter Three
Xiomara

My boss was a huge hijo de puta. I found myself repeating the phrase every time he appeared in my line of vision throughout the week. He was always barking at me for one thing or another, and always over trivial fucking things.

I worked my fucking ass off to get shit right. I didn't want to fuck up another job, least of all before payday. My mamá needed the money, and I didn't want to let her down again. So I gritted my teeth and forced the anger down every time it threatened to rise.

A part of me wanted to snap back at him, but a bigger part of me wanted to fold into myself and disappear.

I didn't do well with criticism. It was stupid, since I'd been criticized my entire life by people who mattered more than him, and yet that didn't stop me from working hard to impress the asshole.

But nothing seemed good enough.

It never was.

Especially today.

Because... I'd fucked up.

"Get your shit and get the fuck out," he growled.

JADE HERNÁNDEZ

I'd never seen Ink look so pissed. Granted, I didn't know him well enough aside from scowls and barked orders, but he'd never been this angry.

"I don't know what happened—"

"You fucked up is what happened."

"I didn't! I swear, I logged their names and times separately into the calendar—"

"You double-booked." His thick brows were drawn together in a line of disapproval. Of anger.

All week I'd been tripping to keep up with his commands. I'd been careful. I was *sure* of it. I was positive I hadn't double-booked. But the evidence was staring us in the face in the form of two clients waiting for tattoos from him.

At the same fucking time.

"Ink, I promise—"

"Your promises mean nothing. Get your shit and leave. I told you if you fucked up, you were gone."

I stood stunned before him for a moment. I had no idea what to do, how to react. What to even do. I was sure I'd logged the correct info in. I was positive.

"Ink, I *know* I did it right."

He sighed, leaning back on the balls of his feet. I hated that there were people around us to witness this. I hated that he didn't seem to give a single fuck that there was an audience bearing witness to my humiliation.

His hand swept over his face, but he didn't look at me with a single ounce of empathy. "You're fired," he said slowly.

Tears pricked behind my eyelids, but I refused to let them fall. "I need this job."

Fer appeared from behind the wall, but I could barely look at her. She'd told me not to fuck up, and I did exactly what she'd advised against. I didn't want to look at her and see the evidence of another person disappointed in me.

"Ink—"

"Not now, Fer."

"Ink—"

"Not now!" he screamed. Then he looked back at me. "If you needed this job so badly, you wouldn't have fucked it up. Now get out of my sight."

He turned from me, leaving me standing there, feeling smaller than I'd ever felt before. That familiar sadness crept through me, embarrassment staining my cheeks. But most of all, there was anger. The anger that had gotten me fired from my last job. The anger that changed me completely and turned me into someone else entirely.

But...

This man was part of an MC, and it was only because of that I was able to tamp those feelings down. I had no idea what they were involved in. What *he* was involved in. What he was capable of.

And I had more pride than throwing a fit in front of so many strangers.

Fuck this place.

Fuck Ink.

With a deep breath, I squared my shoulders and turned. The clients I'd allegedly double-booked stared at me, one with sympathy, the other with a malicious grin.

Asshole.

I ignored them both and grabbed my bag from under the desk, slung it over my shoulder, and walked out of Devil's Ink. The harsh sun was like a slap to the face. It burned the makeup onto my cheeks, marking my face red. This would be nothing compared to the verbal lashing my mamá would give me, though.

Just the thought of seeing disappointment bleed through her dark eyes made me fear going home. The first few times I'd lost jobs and was unable to help the family, she'd lashed out in the only way she knew how. But violence never scared me, and a part of me wondered if the darkness I fostered inside was a gift she'd passed to me when I was in the womb.

After she learned to temper her knee-jerk reactions, she began showing her displeasure in other ways. In ways that hurt more than a slap or a hair pull ever could.

There was just something about her sadness that cut deeper.

Seeing it twice within the span of two weeks was going to ruin me.

I wouldn't tell her.

I decided on that course of action as I walked to the bus stop and hailed a combi in the opposite direction of my house. With my brother using the family car, I was stuck on public transport for the foreseeable future. Maybe I could walk around Tlaxcala City and see if anywhere was hiring. Maybe I'd be lucky enough to land a job before the day was out and I wouldn't have to lie to my mamá.

I stopped in the bustling city's center and used what little extra change I had to buy a BonIce from a man passing by with his cooler and blue penguin uniform. Sucking on the cherry flavored ice through the tube of plastic, I wandered, slipping into several locales to ask if they were hiring.

The problem with looking the way that I did was that people were reluctant to be honest. They were even more reluctant to hire me. So even as I filled out the forms and left, I wondered if they slipped my applications into the trash the moment my back was turned.

It was why working at a tattoo shop had been ideal. I didn't have to worry about anyone judging me for the clothes I wore or the single tattoo on my arm. All I had to worry about was not fucking up.

Unfortunately, I was destined for stupidity. And by the time the day ended, I'd had no luck in snagging a single fucking offer. I got on a combi and then walked three blocks to my house. It was dark, and I was starving.

"Hola, ma," I called out. I took my shoes off at the entrance of the house, slipping into my sandals.

Our house was a dilapidated structure of chipped and molding stone. The once-orange walls bore the evidence of years of summer storms leaking through rock and damaging the paint. Only the richer people could afford to buy the special varnish to get rid of the mold.

We weren't rich.

Our ceiling was nothing but laminated sheets, held down on the top with heavy bricks. Water leaked through when it rained. When it was cold, we huddled beneath our tiger blankets, but even the heavy material wasn't enough to keep it away, and when it was hot, it scorched.

I'd learned to not envy the rich, though, and I didn't hate my house. I knew my mamá had worked hard to give us all she could after my piece of shit papá went to the U.S.A. to send money back, only to never come back at all.

At least I had a roof over my head and my own room.

"Mija, are you hungry?"

My mamá was already in the kitchen heating up tortillas on a comal. Nobody else was around–likely retired to their bedrooms given the late hour–so the food was obviously for me. She didn't even need to wait for me to answer before she pulled out a plate.

"What'd you make?" I slid into the seat at the table.

"Frijoles," she answered. "And eggs with green beans."

My stomach gave a growl. A simple meal, but there was something comforting about it. Funny how I thought that now that I was older. How food I'd gagged over when I was a kid was something I'd learned to appreciate later on, if only because now I knew the struggles and what it took to put food on the table. But also, it tasted like nostalgia.

My mamá sat across from me as I started digging into my meal.

"How was work?" she asked.

I swallowed down the green bean that threatened to turn to lead in my throat. "It was good."

"Is your boss still giving you a hard time?" The scowl was evident in her voice.

"He's starting to act a bit nicer," I lied with ease, scooping beans up with my tortilla. It was easier to stare down at my plate and avoid her gaze than to face her.

"That's good, mija. I'm tired."

I looked up then, noting the dark circles under her eyes. My mamá ran a small kitchen a few blocks away, selling comida corrida to people passing by. It did okay, but it meant she was constantly on her feet cooking. Working hard to earn money to help put food on the table.

Food I was consuming but not contributing to, because I'd gotten fired and probably wouldn't be paid for the days I had worked, considering how angry Ink was when I'd left.

My heart began hurting and I put my tortilla down. "Go to sleep, ma," I said. "I'll clean the kitchen up."

"Are you sure?"

"Yeah. It's okay. I won't be long."

She smiled and stood up, her knees creaking with the action. She groaned as she turned away and made a slow walk towards her room.

All the while I could only stare at her back and gnaw hard on my bottom lip until I tasted blood.

Chapter Four
Ink

The day got worse from the moment I kicked Xiomara out of the shop. Because she'd double-booked, I had Fer helping with stencils and prepping, more clients gathered at the front waiting impatiently for piercings or to make appointments.

It was so chaotic, I ended up sending for a club brother to come help. Cubano came in, a shit-eating grin on his stupid, pretty face. Not in the mood to deal with his bullshit, I immediately put him to work alongside Fer.

Having him there helped move things along, and yet I couldn't shake the nervous feeling that trembled through my blood.

I liked having things in order. Everything had a place, everyone had a task. I couldn't stand plans being upheaved or specific tasks being fucked up.

I knew whatever my club brothers whispered about me. I knew everyone thought I was a fucking nightmare to work with.

Me vale un pepino.

I was organized amidst their chaos. Anyone who wasn't up to par got the boot.

Still, the nervous feeling stayed with me throughout the day. When the final client up and left, Cubano locked the shop doors, and I began my meticulous cleaning routine.

The backs of my shoulder blades began burning and I cracked my neck, turning to see Fer glaring at me.

"Not now," I snapped.

"Yes, now."

Cubano appeared, leaning against the wall, flashing white teeth in a wide smile as he stared back and forth between Fer and I.

Bastardo.

"You fired Xiomara." Fer glared like she meant to kill me with a look.

"Because she fucked up."

Her head shook back and forth. "You're such an idiot. Like, your head is so far up your own ass, there's no oxygen going to that tiny brain of yours."

I frowned. "I'm still your boss," I reminded her. "I can still fire you."

She scoffed. "You won't because I'm the only one within a twenty kilometer radius that'll work for your grumpy ass. Now, if you'll actually listen to me, you'll know that Xiomara didn't fuck up and double book your clients."

I wanted to roll my eyes. "You like her. You'll say anything to get her re-hired."

"Baboso. Your stupid fucking system short-circuited and fucked up. Not her."

Cubano laughed like he was watching a movie unfold before him. I fought hard to ignore my club hermano. He was such a chismosa I knew he was going to take this back and the whole MC was going to know what happened today.

They loved to rattle me. To see me lose my cool.

I didn't want to give them the satisfaction.

I gritted my teeth. "My system is fine."

Fer sighed. "Guess I'll have to show you, then." She whirled, making her way to the front computer.

I had no other choice but to follow. My neck started itching just entertaining her.

"I noticed when I was booking people earlier and doing shit that's below my pay grade. Look." She wiggled the mouse and opened up our calendar app.

I stared at the screen. "What the fuck?"

"Exactly." I could hear the smugness in her voice. "The entire calendar is blank." She pressed the refresh button and the app started wigging out, and suddenly colors appeared over the dates. "Look. It's all fucked up. Appointments got rearranged. Your cloud hasn't been synced to the app so the appointments haven't popped up. So if it's anyone's fault, it's yours."

"Oh, that's rich." Cubano laughed.

I rocked back on the backs of my heels, breathing heavily through my nostrils.

Fuck.

Fuck, fuck, fuck.

She was right.

Xiomara had told me she had done it right, but I'd ignored her. To be fair, her track record didn't give me any sort of confidence that she knew how to do basic tasks. And the app had never failed me before, so how was I supposed to know that it hadn't been her fault?

Fer whirled, glaring at me once again. "You fired her, *humiliated* her, in front of clients."

I had.

I wasn't sure I regretted it. This was a business, after all, and she'd gone around nervously all week like a skittish mouse acting like I was going to step on her.

"Well, it is unfortunate." I didn't want to admit that I was wrong.

"Unfortunate," Fer echoed with disbelief. "You know what?" She grabbed her phone, fingers flying across the screen. A moment later, my own cell beeped with a message. "I texted you her address. Go apologize and hire her back."

Why do I have to do that? The words stuck in my throat.

Fuck.

I liked to run things smoothly. I liked everything to be fucking perfect. That included myself. Just the thought that I'd fucked up didn't sit right with me, but I also had to recognize that when things got messed up, I needed to fix them.

So I would.

But, fuck, Xiomara had stared at me like she wanted to stab me in the balls. She wouldn't accept my apology.

Regardless, it was something I had to do.

I shut off my motorcycle, sitting back in the seat and staring up at the house I parked in front of. My brows furrowed and I pulled out my phone to double check that Fer had given me the right address.

Yup.

This was where Xiomara lived.

The house was... tiny. I wasn't surprised; a lot of houses were, actually. It was nothing new. People worked with what they had.

With a sigh, I threw my leg over my bike and went up towards the house. There was no doorbell, so I rapped my knuckles in quick succession across the door.

I knew it was late, and I prayed she was awake. I could have waited to do this tomorrow, but I didn't want to. My nerves wouldn't let me wait so long.

I waited a minute.

Then two.

Then five...

Finally, the locks on the other side of the door clicked and the door swung open to reveal Xiomara herself.

She was in a government-issued free t-shirt, a green logo on the front of the tattered thing that let me know it was old and well-worn. She wore sleep shorts, leaving her long legs bare.

I was surprised to see very little ink on her skin, and for a second I itched for my tattoo gun so I could put something beautiful on her thighs.

I forced my gaze away from her legs to look up at her face. It was jarring to see her without the makeup I'd grown accustomed to in such a short time. She looked younger. More vulnerable.

Her glare was the same, though.

"What are you doing here?" she demanded.

I hadn't rehearsed what I was going to say, but I didn't need to. There was no use dancing around the subject.

"You didn't fuck up," I said. "It was the system."

She pressed her shoulder against the door frame and crossed her arms against her chest. Even with the small porch light glowing down on her, I could make out the outline of her breasts beneath the shirt. No bra. Nipples poking against the fabric.

Fuck.

"So? What are you doing here?"

"You didn't fuck up. I'm hiring you back."

She blinked, as if she couldn't believe what it was she was hearing. I had never expected to be put in this position, so I understood. I never gave second chances. She was lucky she was getting this at all.

"So from what I'm hearing, it was your fault and you owe me an apology?"

I would have glowered harder at her had it not been for the mischievous gleam in her eye. Had she just cracked a joke?

I fought the urge to shift uncomfortably. "Do you want the job or not?"

She straightened at the brisk tone but eventually sighed and nodded. I could hardly see with the lone lamplight, but maybe I imagined the color rising on her cheeks.

What I didn't imagine was a wall slamming closed behind her eyes and that mischievous glint vanishing, replaced by something almost shy and demure instead.

A complete turn from what she'd been like before.

"Okay," she whispered. "I'd like the job back, please."

I nodded and then stood there.

Awkward beats passed between us and neither of us said a thing. I should have turned around and walked back to my bike, but something about the woman beneath the light was fucking hypnotizing.

The cutting, sharp points of her thick brows, the fierce angled edges of her eyes.

She was beautiful, of course; I'd fucking known that the moment I saw her. But there was something particularly mesmerizing about her right then. Stripped of the makeup she wore like armor, she looked different, and I hated how much that captivated me.

"Right." I took a step backwards. "See you tomorrow."

She started to close the door, but a voice filtered outside.

"Xiomara, who is that at this hour?"

An older woman appeared from behind her. Wrapped in a shawl to protect herself from the night chill, her graying hair frizzed around her forehead and cheeks. There were wrinkle lines around her eyes, the creases of her skin pulling her expression down into one of displeasure.

She glared at me, her eyes taking me in the way the señoras always did. With judgment. Disdain.

That was normal, and I didn't take it personally.

"Who is this?" the woman demanded.

"Ma, this is my boss," Xiomara introduced slowly.

Her eyes cut to me, and in them I read the note of panic.

I wondered if she'd told her mamá I'd fired her. Probably not. I wouldn't mention it.

"Buenas noches, señora," I greeted. "Sorry if I woke you. I was just telling Xiomara that I would pick her up for work tomorrow."

Her mamá looked suspiciously at me. "This late? You couldn't phone her instead?"

"I don't have her number, I'm afraid." I hadn't bothered putting it into my contact list, thinking she wouldn't last the week.

Her mamá looked at me like I was a liar.

"Ah, right." Xiomara rattled off her number, and I immediately punched it into my phone before pocketing the device.

I nodded. "Thank you. And sorry again for disturbing your night."

Taking a ride back to the club house, I enjoyed the wind whipping against my face, letting the flow clear my mind, but it kept going back to Xiomara.

I'd not pretend I didn't feel anything other than guilt, especially when I prided myself on being immaculate.

I'd given her the job back, and I'd noted her relief, but I'd also noted her living conditions.

She appeared to live like most upper-lower class Mexicans. But if she desperately needed a job, I wondered why she couldn't seem to hold one down.

I should have asked. I suddenly needed to know that information.

Maybe it was my guilt that drove my next action. It didn't matter. But when I arrived at the club house, I waved over a prospect.

"You're coming with me tomorrow," I ordered. No need for politeness. Prospects were our bitches. "But I need you to go buy a few supplies first."

Chapter Five
Xiomara

It was bizarre knowing my boss—who I'd mentally called an hijo de puta many times—was picking me up for work.

I was grateful that he hadn't mentioned anything to my mamá. If she would've known he fired me only to rehire me, she would've taken a belt to my back or glared at me in disappointment for the lies I spewed.

Still, the next day I dressed with more care than usual.

For some fucking reason.

Not like I was trying to impress that asshole.

But I was grateful for the second chance. So I took care pencilling in my brows and darkening my liner, lining and filling my lips red. I took a toothbrush to my edges, pressing and curling the hairs against my cheeks and forehead.

My hoops went in last before I admired myself in my mirror. My band shirt, a hand-me-down that was too big for my curvy frame, belonged to my brother. A tighter, white, long sleeved shirt went beneath that and tan pants with a black belt completed my ensemble. My converse were frayed and coming apart. They were one of the first gifts my papá had sent from the other side before he stopped calling altogether.

JADE HERNÁNDEZ

I would've tossed them out of pure spite if I hadn't needed them so badly. Shoes in Mexico were expensive, and the ones that didn't cost around thousands of pesos were made of cheap, ugly material.

The first thing I was going to do–if I survived until payday–was shoe shop.

My mamá was in the kitchen when I went downstairs, tying a checkered apron behind her waist.

"Buenos dias," I greeted.

She was looking out the window. "Who is that in front of our house? Is that your boss?"

My heart pounded and I snapped my gaze outside. Sure enough, Ink was there, climbing off his bike. I hadn't heard him arrive. There was a truck there too, and a man hopped out and went to the back, pulling things out of the bed of the vehicle.

I went to open the door before they could knock.

"You're early." The words felt like an accusation on my lips, and I regretted the tone immediately.

I shouldn't piss him off when I knew how volatile his moods were.

But he didn't mention it. Just nodded his head.

"I brought a prospect."

"Okay?"

We stared at one another for a tense moment. I wasn't sure why he brought a prospect, and I should've asked, yet I couldn't tear my gaze away from Ink's.

Something felt... different since he hired me back. It was only a few moments in which we'd interacted, and yet something phenomenal had shifted between the two of us. Maybe it was his own guilt driving him. He wasn't kinder, but he hadn't actively growled at me when he came over yesterday. And now, there was something softer around the edges of his eyes. Not too soft, of course, and he was still an asshole.

The longer we stared, the more my heart began beating faster and faster until I couldn't stand the anxiety.

But still, I refused to look away.

It wasn't until a man shuffled up behind him. "Where do you want me, Ink?"

Ink spoke first. "Can we come inside?"

I should have said no. No need to expose my mamá to them any more than need be. No need to dawdle either.

But I found myself moving aside and letting them through.

I went after them, awkward in my own home, as the prospect stopped in the living room. For the first time, I noticed he carried with him bags from the paint store.

"Um…what is that for?"

"The prospect is going to paint your walls."

I blinked at Ink.

What the fuck?

Just then my ma came in, fussing with her hair in front of company, but pursing her lips in displeasure.

"Buenos dias," she greeted, though she looked like she'd sucked on a lemon.

"Buenos dias, señora," Ink greeted politely, moving to take her hand and press a kiss to her cheek. The prospect did the same.

It was very surreal.

"What's all this?" my ma asked, staring with mistrust at the bags on the floor and the men in her living room.

"We came to fix the walls," Ink declared.

He didn't ask permission, either. He just... commanded, and he commanded the room with his very essence.

My ma started to bristle.

"Then they'll be repainted. The prospects will finish in about a week, sooner if they can."

"They?"

He looked at me, gaze piercing. "We have several prospects."

Okay?

The prospect in question began pulling the supplies out of the bag, a small tin can of that special varnish to kill the mold on the walls and the special brush and face mask.

"Hold on," my ma demanded. "How much is this going to cost?"

For real. One of those tins went for five hundred a piece. That was a week's worth of groceries, if that. Half a week if we bought meat or chicken.

"No cost, señora. Xiomara is a great employee, and we like to give benefits like this to everyone at no cost to you."

Jesus Christ.

This man didn't lay on charm, but it came across that way regardless. My ma looked at me with furrowed brows.

Surely she thought I was fucking him.

Because I'd only been working for him for a damn week. Hardly enough to warrant this special treatment.

He probably felt really guilty about his fuck up. Why else would he be doing this?

But now my mamá probably thought I was a puta.

"I'm sorry, but we can't accept this," she stated firmly.

"All due respect, señora, I'm not asking."

God, what a dick.

I stepped in between them before my ma could snap at him. I turned to her, grabbing her hand and lowering my voice to a whisper. "What's the problem, mamita? Let them do this for us. Dios knows our walls need the upkeep."

"Xiomara, we don't accept charity."

She'd rather suffer moldy walls and shitty lungs than accept anyone's help. This woman's pride... I understood. I really did.

But Ink was a massive piece of shit, and I figured I'd earned this at least. A signing bonus, so to speak.

"Come on, ma. It's free."

She stared at me, her disdain clear. "At what cost?"

I knew what she was implying. She really did think I was fucking him. Or at least a loose woman. She probably thought this was my one-way ticket to hell.

"Ma..."

She sighed in obvious resignation. "Fine. Let them do it. I have to get to work."

She said her tense goodbyes and then left. Her disappointment in me was viscerally obvious. It choked through me, causing that familiar anxious sensation to rise. I glared at Ink as soon as the door closed behind her. "You realize she thinks I'm blowing you in exchange for this, right?"

The bastard didn't even crack a smile.

The prospect, however, chortled. I finally looked at him, taking him in. He was an attractive dude, I supposed. A little young, maybe a few years older than me. His dark hair was gelled back and his cut didn't have any fanfare except for the single word *Prospect* on it.

His own eyes raked over me and he bit his bottom lip, a leering appreciative gesture. His pierced brows kicked up.

"I mean, if you want to blow someone in exchange for this..."

Ink's entire expression changed then. It darkened, a storm ready to erupt. He whirled so fast, his palm slapping against the prospect's face and shoving him against the wall. There was a resounding crack as the guy's head collided against cement.

"You don't fucking talk to her," Ink threatened. "You don't fucking touch her. Don't even fucking look at her, pendejo. You got that?"

The prospect's reply was muffled against Ink's palm. But the panic was evident in his wide eyes. Ink made a sound of disgust and shoved him away. "Get to fucking work. Your time frame just shortened thanks to that big fucking mouth."

The prospect immediately moved, but he didn't look at me again.

Ink did, the previous expression settling back to the unaffected bastard I'd come to know. Though there was something about the anger that had made a shiver slide down my spine and goosebumps to crawl along my arms.

A tiny, miniscule, puta-ish part of me wanted to know what it felt like to be handled so roughly. To be fucked with my face against a wall just like that.

Another part of me screamed to get a fucking grip.

"Ready?" he asked. As if he hadn't just shoved a dude's head against my wall.

"I can't leave a stranger in my house."

I wasn't born yesterday. People liked to steal irrelevant shit, but stealing was stealing. I wouldn't hear the end of it if someone pilfered one of my ma's recuerdos from a distant cousin's baptism from ten years ago.

"If he touches anything or if anything turns up missing, a speck of paint gets on your belongings, I will personally shoot every fucking finger of his and make him eat the bullets afterwards."

Why did I believe that?

A better question was, why the fuck did that turn me on so much?

"Okay," I said, hating how absolutely breathless I sounded. "Then let's go to work."

There was something about getting on the back of Ink's bike that felt even more intimate than his piercing stare. He waited patiently, quietly, while I stood awkwardly trying to decide if this was a good idea or not.

My body was already having a strange reaction to him. Adding the intimacy of riding a motorcycle together would make my concha cry out like la llorona wailing for children.

Damn.

There went my errant thoughts.

Eventually I did hop on before he could bark at me to do it. Throwing one leg over the bike, I tried to keep a respectful distance between our bodies. He still didn't start the thing, however. He reached an arm behind him and yanked me close by the hem of my shirt until I was practically molded to his back.

"Hold on tight," he ordered in the growling voice of his. The rumbling sound of it sent tiny bursts of delicious, dizzying energy through me. I wrapped my arms around his waist in a daze and then we were off.

My pueblo was a maze of potholes and cobblestone roads, but Ink dodged each one as if he knew them by heart. When he got on the main roads and sped up, I felt a thrill of adrenaline whirl through my insides. The urge to throw my hands up and let out a shout was immediate, but I only held tighter to him. There was something freeing about this, in every possible way.

When we finally pulled to a slow stop, my heart was racing and my wind-whipped hair ratted down my shoulders. But I didn't care about that. Laughter filled me as I hopped off the bike.

"That was fun."

Ink grunted, and the sound pulled me back to my current reality.

He was my boss.

This was my second chance.

I couldn't act like a foolish child and risk losing this job. Again. Yes, he was painting my house, but that felt more like an apology on his end rather than anything else. I knew I had to work extra hard to keep him happy now, regardless of what happened.

I cleared my throat and started across the street towards the shop. It was open, and when we went inside, Fer was sitting behind the desk.

A wide smile broke out on her mouth as soon as she saw me. "You're back!" she squealed. The genuine, excited greeting brought a small smile to my lips. "Good! I told him his shitty system needs an update. I knew it wasn't your fault, amiga."

My face heated at the reminder of said system.

INK

"Let it go, Fer," Ink growled.

"Never. You need to get a new one. Fix it. Something! Anything!" Fer waved her hands through the air, her dyed hair flinging with every exaggerated movement of her body. She was such a character.

But her words reminded me of something, and I wasn't sure...

My mouth dropped open. "I–" I shut up again when Ink's piercing gaze whipped in my direction. Why did he have to stare at me like that? It made me lose all my senses. My breath came out in shallow pants, and I had to force my lungs to expand at a normal fucking rate.

"What?" he asked.

I started to retreat into myself. I shouldn't have opened my stupid mouth. This shop was his baby. It was something he'd been working to perfect for years, right down to the system. I'd only been here a week, but even I could tell the immense pride and work he put into this place. I was nobody to come in and start throwing out ideas. I was on thin ice as it was.

The fact that I knew how badly I needed to keep this job–for my ma and my siblings–diminished my confidence. Or maybe that was a culmination of losing jobs, one right after the other.

"You got an idea? Spit it out," Ink declared, and his voice was tinged with annoyance. "Don't keep quiet when you have something to say."

Bastard. Just when I was starting to think he was decent. It seemed like my mind and vagina weren't on the same wavelength.

"I was going to say that I know an easier way to help with the system. In a way where it won't mess up and double book clients. The calendar app is so easy to get wrong because it relies on the cloud and internet. If your internet goes down, as I suspect was the case with this mix-up, then it'll just happen again."

Ink looked at me differently then; not with anger or annoyance, but with something else that shone in his eyes.

Something that looked a lot like acceptance.

It was too early to tell, but I think I'd just impressed my boss.

"Show me," he said.

Days had passed since *the incident*, which was what I was officially calling what had happened when I got fired and rehired. I'd fallen back into my routine. Payday had come and gone, and I'd put a good amount down to go buy myself some new shoes next payday.

Ink no longer stared at me like I was a useless addition to the shop. Sure, we weren't buddy-buddy, but he wasn't buddy-buddy with anyone. At least he was nicer, smirking at me occasionally when he found it in his icy cold heart to do so. I hated how that smirk made me feel. Like I wanted to preen every time I seemed to do something right in his eyes. Like I was looking for that asshole to praise me.

Newsflash, I wasn't...

Was I?

No, no era eso.

I wasn't sure I wanted to admit it, but I found I was rather enjoying the job. Even if his presence still gave me anxiety.

I was wiping down the surfaces in the shop with a rag and disinfectant when the front door opened. The entire place smelt of lemon and it made my nose twitch.

I set aside the rag and turned at the desk. Every cell in my body froze.

Something cautious, born from years of being a woman in a machista country, rose up inside me. Where men catcalled you even if you wore pajamas and a messy bun. Where men leaned out car windows to slap your ass only to peel off in a cloud of smoke and raucous laughter while you were left to deal with the violation.

We were always told not to wear skirts, to not provoke. There were scarier things than monsters that roamed the shadows of the streets.

So I knew. Immediately I knew that the men before me were *not* nice people.

They weren't Mexican, or even Latine for that matter, with their too light skin tone and burnt noses. I knew we came in all colors, the remnants of European blood flowing through our veins, but one could usually tell when someone wasn't local or didn't quite belong.

"Good evening," the man in the front of the pack said. He took off his shades, revealing crisp, blue eyes. Like chips of ice. He smirked and spoke in an accent.

He was wearing a stuffy suit in the heat. I knew he had to be sweating buckets under there.

"Can I help you?" My tone was droll.

His eyes raked over me, making me uncomfortable, though I'd never show it on the outside. I took a breath, eyeing the bat Fer kept behind the desk on the floor.

At first, I'd thought that thing was a decoration, meant to be mounted on the walls alongside the instruments and artistic paraphernalia. When I'd asked about it, Fer just shook her head, hair bouncing against her rouged cheeks.

"People don't fuck with Los Diablos," she said. "But you can never be too careful."

And there the bat stayed, a ghost of a companion behind the desk beside me.

It lay just within reach and out of sight from the people on the opposite side.

"Is your boss around, pretty thing?"

My brow lifted, mocking his condescending tone. "Do you have an appointment?"

The slight tick of his jaw that I didn't rush to find Ink let me know he was annoyed.

"I don't need one."

"Everyone needs one."

One of the white goonies in the back pushed forward, the aggression in his movements making me tense. "Just call your boss to the front, *puta*."

The accented way he butchered the insult made me want to sigh.

"You gringos and your privilege," I said, surprising them with my own perfect English. Their eyes widened and I smirked. What? A brown woman in Mexico couldn't speak English? I wanted to laugh in their faces at that bias. "You always want things done as soon as you order it. Understand, no one sees Ink without an appointment, got it?"

What I didn't tell them was that Ink wasn't in. Neither was Fer. They'd gone to a local class to teach piercings and tattoos, but they wouldn't be long. I opened to clean and set appointments. They still had afternoon clients to see. I just hoped the silence in the back wasn't so glaringly obvious.

The angry goon looked like he wanted to reach for me, maybe strangle me.

For a moment the darker side of me wanted it. *Fuck with me and find out, gringo pendejo.*

But the leader of the bunch put a hand to his chest and they stepped back.

"You tell Ink we stopped by."

"And *who* are you exactly?"

"He'll know who we are."

And with that, they left.

It wasn't ten minutes later that Ink and Fer came into the shop. I was still at the counter breathing heavily when they arrived, chasing away the darkness that threatened to cloud my vision. But chasing nightmares was hard, and it was no wonder that those who did it were too afraid to dream.

Ink took one look at me and demanded, "What's wrong?"

It was like wading through fog, and his voice was a beacon of light that I tried my damndest to get to. I recounted the events, my voice steady, though my heart thumped hard in my chest. Ink stepped in front of me, using his fingers to grasp my chin and tilt my head up.

"Did they hurt you?" he snarled.

I took a breath. His anger was like a balm to my soul, and it chased my own feelings away enough so that I could look into his eyes as I answered, "No."

"But they frightened you."

I didn't say anything, not because I was afraid I'd appear weak, but because I was afraid I'd sound like a total loca. He let out a curse. "Xiomara, whenever anyone comes in and pulls shit like that, you call me immediately. I don't give a fuck if I'm teaching a class or tattooing in the back. You tell me and I will come."

I felt it. A promise of protection I somehow knew would never be broken. I swallowed tightly as I nodded.

"Okay."

"Fer, watch her. I need to call Loco."

He left, taking the heat with him as he dug into his pockets and fished out his phone. His presence was replaced with Fer's, her eyes soft with concern.

"Are you okay?" she asked.

"Who's Loco?"

"The president of Los Diablos."

"Why is he going to call him?"

Fer offered me a smile. "That's club business. I bet the guys that came in were looking to start beef with Los Diablos. They always target the businesses first, but don't worry. The club will protect us."

"Does this happen often?" I resisted the urge to remind her that she was the one who told me nobody was stupid enough to fuck with the MC. It appeared as though someone stupid had definitely arrived to shake shit up, and I'd been caught on the warning's end.

"They haven't had any problems in a while, and it's not as common as you think. Are you worried? Are you going to quit?"

Her panicked expression made me offer up a small smile. "No," I said, and there was a truth to my words that settled down to my bones. "I'm not worried."

Chapter Six
Ink

Those gringos hijos de puta.

The minute Xiomara described the situation to me I knew exactly who we were dealing with.

I made a call to Loco, and after he finished cussing them out down the line, he told me to get to the clubhouse immediately so we could deal with the threat.

But first I had to get Fer and Xiomara home.

"We're closing shop," I announced as I walked back to the front.

Fer nodded, already familiar with shit even if she didn't know details. "My brother is on his way."

"Xiomara, I'm taking you home."

She didn't argue or protest. I watched as she calmly sent out texts from the shop phone to let our clients know that their appointments were canceled. I'd make it up to them somehow, probably by offering a discount, but club shit always took precedence over everything else.

We waited until Fer's brother picked her up and then hopped on my bike. Unlike the first time, I didn't have to demand she hold me tightly. Her body molded itself onto mine like she was meant there.

JADE HERNÁNDEZ

I didn't stop to think about how this was the second time Xiomara had been on the back of my bike. Just like I didn't think about how she'd been the *only* woman on the back of my bike *ever*. There was significance in the gesture, one I didn't want to think too hard on when there were more important things to worry about at the moment.

We didn't take long to get to her place. She jumped off, but before she could leave, my hand shot out to grasp at her hip and held her in place. She froze, her eyes searching my own.

"Lock your door, Xiomara," I ordered.

"I will," she assured me.

"And if there's anyone wandering around that shouldn't be–"

"I'll let you know." She nodded her head.

"Good girl."

The words left my lips and made an immediate flush crawl up her face.

"Go inside," I ordered, a growl snapping from me without meaning to. I didn't need her flushing face making my dick hard, but it was already too fucking late.

I wasn't quite sure when it had happened. My dick stirred ever since I hired her back. Every time she was in the room, it came alive, like she was the one I'd been waiting for. I tried to tame that primal part of me, though. She was my fucking employee. Fucking employees ensured for a messy work environment. There were club putas for that type of thing. I could rub one out or fuck one of them to get Xiomara out of my system.

Especially because she'd proved far more competent than I thought her to be originally.

My dick liked competence, apparently.

Fuck.

Xiomara whipped around and rushed up the path towards her house. Only once she was locked inside did I peel out of there and head towards the clubhouse.

It was chaos when I arrived.

I caught up to Loco.

My president was an erratic bastard whose name fit him to a fucking T. Tattoos swirled across most of his skin, crawling up his neck and near the corners of his eyes. His bald head all but shone against the light of the setting sun, his manic, angry gaze snapping over our brothers rushing through the clubhouse.

"Ink, what the fuck took you so long?" he demanded.

"I had to take Xiomara home."

"Well, we moved our product."

Our guns.

We'd been having issues with those fucking gringos moving into our territory, acting like they could take over the local gun trade. They didn't just dabble in that, either. They were trying to get involved in the skin trade and take over the streets of Tlaxcala too.

We worked directly with out-of-state gangs like the Raven Brothers and local cartels. At least, with the ones that ran drugs and guns. We didn't fuck with skin traders. So them trying to bring that shit into our territory?

They'd been trying to get us into their operation for a while now. We'd declined, but they'd gotten more aggressive in their insistence, because they knew they needed our permission to move their shit in Diablos territory.

Them coming to my place of business looking for me, subtly threatening Xiomara, was all but an act of war.

And for that, they'd fucking burn.

And Los Diablos would watch them, cackling through the flames.

Chapter Seven
Xiomara

Ink was in and out of the shop, though more out than in, for the following days. "Club shit," he'd muttered before making me hold most of his appointments and leaving Fer and I alone.

I'd looked to Fer, but she'd just shrug and say that it was normal.

"Women aren't supposed to know what goes on with the club," she said. "Especially us. We aren't anything except employees. Even the Old Ladies aren't privy to their insider information."

I knew the Old Ladies were their wives. Or something similar to that. And I didn't even want to know what Los Diablos were up to. The less I knew, the better. I had enough to worry about at home, like making enough money to help pay for gas, electricity, and food without adding their bullshit into the mix.

I just hoped that Ink was going to be able to pay me, what with him canceling on so many clients and what not. I figured it wasn't something he did often–if ever–judging by their surprise every time I had to call them to break the news.

Still, the sparse times I saw him were in the mornings and at nights, when he drove me home on the back of his bike. It happened every night without fail. He wouldn't say a single word about his day, though I could tell by the bags beneath his eyes that it had been grueling. He'd just lift that dark, heavy helmet in my direction and wait for me to take it. We'd arrive at my place in about fifteen minutes, where I'd numbly get off, hand him back his helmet, and he'd nod.

Those were the extent of our interactions.

Ink was cold by nature, and even so it was something familiar to me. Had he been flirtatious, I would have been kicked to the curb long ago. I'd dealt with too many bosses like that, and I was glad Ink was different.

At closing, I waited for Ink behind the desk, scrolling through my phone to pass the time.

"Ey." Fer drew my attention towards her. "My brother is waiting for me. You good?"

"Yeah, just waiting on Ink."

"Want us to wait till he gets here?"

"Nah, no te preocupes. He won't be long."

Fer looked unsure, hesitating and rocking on the backs of her heels.

I shot her a look. "Go. I know you guys take a combi and the last one leaves soon."

Combis were cheaper than taxis. Why pay a taxi around a hundred when you could pay eight pesos a person? The only problem was, transport stopped at around nine, ten at the latest.

Fer nodded. "Alright, well, I'll see you later."

I waved her off and went back to scrolling and shooting the shit with my online Latine community. I wasn't always able to be active on the forums, but when I was, I liked to reply and catch up on everything I missed.

INK

Nonconsequential things were always traded back and forth. Things like how to press edges, make chilito quemado, and there were even groups asking for beta readers for poetry and books.

I was so engrossed in my task–looking over the written lyrics from one of the members named Veronica who wanted to be a singer one day–I didn't realize how much time passed after that. By the time I did, it was late, and Ink still hadn't shown up. It was weird, but maybe there was club stuff going on. No texts, though. As I began typing one up to ask him when he was coming, the door to the shop opened.

I looked up and my fingers froze on the screen of my phone.

"Hello, *puta*."

My lip pulled up at the sight of the gringos from a few days ago. They were back, still dressed immaculately in those pretty little suits of theirs, but this time there were no niceties on their expressions.

An immediate chill went down my back and my thumb pressed down on the send button. I set my phone down in front of me and dropped my hands to the side.

"What do you want?" I asked.

In unison, they smirked.

"So you do remember us? That's very good. Because we'd like for you to give a message to your boss."

JADE HERNÁNDEZ

There was a single moment when the darkness swallowed me whole. I couldn't be sure how long it lasted, only that it did and by the time it was over, it spat me back out into the light.

My breaths sawed in and out of my body, painfully scraping through my throat every time I tried to suck in air. My face was coated in thick liquid, causing me to see red.

I tasted copper on my lips, and while I still had my sense of taste, everything else was numb. The pain in my body didn't come until later. The rest of my senses came gradually. Sound. White noise filled with my own breaths. Red became the maroon and black decor of the shop. My eye throbbed. My knuckles screamed. Every bone in my body felt like it'd been through a grinder.

And yet the sweet breath of life filled me.

"Fucking *shit*! Xiomara! Xiomara, are you okay?"

I vaguely recognized the voice. Not at first. Not until he stood in front of me, taking my bloodied cheeks in his hands.

My breathing finally stilled and his name escaped me on a sigh of relief. "Ink."

His cold facade cracked like ice splintering down the middle. The veins on his neck pulsed. His jaw worked. And yet his eyes on me were tender.

"Xiomara, are you okay?"

"I'm fine. I think."

"Baby, let go of the bat."

I hadn't felt the cold metal grasped tightly in my hands, slick with rivulets of blood. I loathed to let the weapon go, but Ink was here.

He was safe.

It'd be okay.

The bat dropped between us with a clang to the ground.

Only then did Ink grip me by the elbows and turn me. The jolting action pulled me from my shock, like every other time before I felt myself grounded back to reality after the initial disorientation. Everything slammed into me at once. The smell was the worst of all. The tang-like cold metal.

My gaze swept around the shop, surveying the destruction.

"Let's get out of here," Ink ordered. "I'll take care of you."

"But what about–"

"The club will handle it," he assured me as he walked me out of Devil's Ink.

And I believed him.

I believed he would handle the mess–and the dead bodies–I left on the floor of his shop.

Chapter Eight
Xiomara

I BARELY REMEMBERED THE ride on the back of Ink's bike. I only knew the wind on my face and the blur of buildings and cornfields as we sped across the highway. When he finally stopped, that numb state had almost completely dissipated and in its place was shame.

I thought I was done with that.

The rage.

The kind that morphed me into a different person entirely and made me black out and forget myself, like someone who'd shot back too much tequila. There were blank spaces for a while until memories rushed back in flashes.

Of my hands closing around a bat and striking heads. Of the pain of being struck, kicked, beaten, only to get back up again and give them what they deserved.

But this time, I'd gone too far.

I tried to see if guilt would settle, and I think that was what shamed me most of all. It didn't exist. I didn't give a fuck that I'd killed those men. They deserved it.

Was I a broken human because of it? Would Ink recoil from me now?

He didn't. He took my hand and pulled me towards a two story home behind a stone wall with electric wire circling the top. I barely glanced at the place. Even as he took me inside.

Even as I heard a small gasp and Ink's reply, "Go back to sleep, ma. She's fine."

And then I was being pushed to a seat.

I reacted, taking in a breath and looking around. I was obviously in Ink's room. If the dark decor was of any indication.

He moved about with confidence and determination before he kneeled in front of me between my open legs.

Silently, he took my hands and swept a wet cloth over my split knuckles. I didn't even wince at the sting.

"Fuck, Xiomara," Ink rumbled. "What happened?"

It was spoken like an order. A command.

He wanted the truth, and he'd get it. One way or another.

I waited until he finished wiping the blood clean from one hand and started on the other before I spoke.

"They came in looking to leave you a message through me."

His grip tightened on my hand at those words.

"So I defended myself."

This earned me a chuckle, one I was surprised to hear come from his lips. "I can see that..."

"The bodies...I can't go to jail. My mamá needs me. She needs money. She's getting on in years."

"You aren't going to jail, Xiomara."

I stared doubtfully at him. "Last time I checked, killing someone–let alone three someones–lands you in prison."

"Loco is going to take care of it. They're cleaning up the bodies as we speak, plus Los Diablos have the police in our pockets. No one is going to arrest you. You aren't going to prison."

"Are you sure?"

"Yes. You're safe."

Tension eased from my shoulders. Good. Los Diablos would protect me. I believed in that. In him.

"Xiomara..." Ink lowered one of my hands and reached the rag up to swipe the blood from my face. Even in that he was tender and I winced when he went near my eye. "Why did you get fired from your last job?"

Another demand.

I wanted to look away but he commanded my attention until I became lost in him. "My manager felt me up behind the counter," I confessed. "And then... I blacked out." At his questioning look, I elaborated. "There's a rage inside me, Ink. It turns me into a different person. Into someone who beats three grown men to death with a bat. I beat my manager up. He didn't die, but I wished he had."

I whispered my confession, wondering if I'd see disgust in Ink's face. He dropped the rag and cupped my cheek. What I saw in his face wasn't disgust.

It was reverence.

"I'm sorry my club dragged you into our shit. I promise, I'll keep you safe from now on. No one will ever mark your skin again." His hands caressed my body, electrifying every single nerve inside me. "Only I get to do that. With ink."

My heart sped up. No one had promised me security before. I was independent enough to know I could care for myself, but also self-aware enough to know that I'd craved those words.

"And if you want to quit, I understand."

My hands clamped against his wrists, tightening despite the ache it caused. "No," I said. "Please. My family needs me to bring money in."

"Okay." His thumbs swiped across my cheeks. "I promise you, Los Diablos has your back. What you did tonight? We will remember this. You will be repaid in full."

My eyes closed in relief as Ink pressed his forehead against mine.

He breathed deeply and I did the same. Like we were breathing one another in. Like we could taste the salt of each other's souls, hear the rhythm of our hearts and somehow sync them together.

My heart calmed in his presence, content, and something low in my gut coiled at the proximity. Something new. His promises of protection and sincerity washed over me.

Something I never thought I'd crave until I had it before me. The air shifted. My skin felt electrified, and when I opened my eyes, it was to find him already staring at me.

"I want to kiss you," he whispered.

The confession felt forbidden in the space between us, and the words startled me, if only because I never imagined him saying them, but they were exactly what I wanted. What I'd craved for the longest time. Perhaps I hadn't even realized it until right then.

"Yes."

He leaned close, his lips grazing mine a fraction. The scrape of his beard against my skin. A sigh left me and I leaned closer, waiting for that first touch... just for Ink to pull back.

"I can't, though."

I blinked in confusion.

What–

"You're my employee."

That statement pulled pain into me. I couldn't shake it, but I knew he was right. No matter how disappointed a part of me was for that fact.

Maybe it was the moment, the adrenaline crashing from the day. All I knew was that this was a bad idea. He was my boss and we had no business starting something neither of us could finish.

I pulled away. "Can you take me home?"

If he was taken aback by my abrupt request, he didn't say anything. He took my hand silently and we both stood up.

I couldn't breathe clearly until he dropped me off at my own place. Even then, I said nothing as I went forward and closed the door behind me.

Thankfully, my mamá didn't wake. Not even as I stripped and hopped in the shower.

I washed the day off and let my tears mingle with the water.

And let my sins roll from my back. Tomorrow would be a new day.

Chapter Nine
Ink

Fuck.

I shouldn't have said a word. But she'd been so close. Drenched in blood, knuckles split, eyes burning with an anger that made my cock go hard.

Her deadly rage was a turn-on. Had I thought competence made my dick hard? I took it back. It was the sight of that goddess of a woman, drenched in blood, filled to the brim with feminine rage, that made me want to drop to my knees and make her my Vieja.

I'd been fighting my urges for a while. Ever since I'd rehired her, I paid more attention. I noticed more. And I'd begun to crave more. And the fraction of a touch I'd given her, my lips touching hers? It only opened the floodgates of desire and made me crave like I'd never craved anything else.

The next day she came into work, even after I'd texted and told her she was allowed to take the day off. When she walked through the shop doors, her gaze settled over the clean floors. The lack of bodies and blood.

I'd promised her Loco would take care of it and he had. He was also sending hermanos by the shop later. I think they were all just curious about what had happened, and they found it hard to believe Xiomara had ended their lives herself with a bat, but the evidence didn't lie.

She ignored me as she placed herself behind the counter and began doing her job. I tried not to let that rejection sting or piss me off, but it did. Especially when Loco came through the door a moment later and stopped in front of her. She must've realized who he was simply by looking at his cuero, but I was sure his appearance was staggering.

My prez looked fresh out of fucking prison.

He whistled low, his eyes taking in the black eye she'd tried to hide behind makeup. "Shiner," he said. Then his gaze raked lower, taking in the whole of her body. I recognized the appreciative gleam in his eyes. "So, you're the one that beat three bitch ass gringos to death with a bat, huh?"

Xiomara cleared her throat. "Um... yeah."

Loco leaned against the top of my desk, smirking at her. "That's hot, nena."

A growl rose in my throat. Possessive, feral, when I had no fucking right to be. I crowded behind her, looming after her tall frame to stare down at my president.

Loco eyed me, then her, then me again, that smirk curling into a knowing smile. "So it's like that, huh?"

"It's exactly like that."

Loco knocked his knuckles against the desk and pushed himself away. "Alright. Well, Xiomara, we are having an asada over at the clubhouse. You went to bat for us–*literally*–so your cute ass better be there. Bring your family, too. Don't worry, though. We won't tell them what you did for us. It'll be our little secret."

Xiomara nodded and Loco shot a devilish smirk in my direction. Even though he was my prez, I'd never wanted to punch him in the face more than I did in that moment.

There was no explanation for why I was getting possessive over her. I'd made it clear the night before that nothing could happen.

No matter how badly I wanted it to.

Chapter Ten
Xiomara

THE DIABLOS CLUBHOUSE WAS packed with people of all types. Some wore cueros, others wore street clothes. Some of the women wore leather with the words *Property of* on the back. So many of them sported tattoos, and a lot of them didn't.

I took it all in with curiosity, while my ma whispered a prayer next to me. This was a culture shock for her, but she'd been nothing but polite so far.

So had everyone else. I guess I hadn't expected everyone to be so welcoming. Loco had been the first to greet me, wrapping me into a hug like we were family. After his initial flirtations at the shop, he didn't hit on me again. It was a damn shame, too. The man was fucking fine. His tattooed face and neck only added to his appeal, and the mischief gleaming in his eyes was endearing and sexy both.

Most of the Diablos, even those I hadn't met, said hi. A lot of them came up to introduce themselves to me. I figured word had gotten out about what I'd done, and instead of the shame that had previously filled me, I felt welcomed. Like I was among people who understood, and instead of being upset, they were proud. They probably wouldn't have even blinked twice if they knew I didn't feel guilty about taking three lives.

Or that I'd do it again if I had to.

We mingled for a while, falling into a sense of camaraderie with the others. I was pulled into the fold of women wearing *Property of* jackets. There weren't many, as it seemed the single men overpowered the clubhouse at the moment. There were other women too, scantily dressed, though gathered together in their own separate circle. I bet they were the putas of the club, girls who slept with them all in exchange for accommodations, food, and work. An interesting life, one I wouldn't judge, no matter how hatefully some of them chose to glare in my direction.

Soon, food and booze flowed and more of the single club members started sidling up to me. I laughed at their jokes, flattered at their interest. It was no secret that I was pretty, I was self-aware enough to know that about myself. I relished in their attention, even if I wished it was Ink instead.

As if I'd summoned the surly tattoo artist, he appeared behind Cubano, a dark-skinned, curly haired Afro-Mexicano with a stunning smile, and gripped him by the back of the collar.

"Get lost." He yanked.

Cubano didn't move. He was a jovial dude and turned those blindingly white teeth in Ink's direction. "Can't you see I'm having a conversation with the lady?"

Ink let out a growl, a sound that was almost animalistic and violent.

It did something to my core.

"Get. Fucking. Lost."

Cubano laughed but did as he was told, winking at me. "Fine," he conceded as he walked away. "I'll take Xio's mom out to dance."

I glared lazily at Ink. "We were talking."

"Not anymore. Come here." He gripped me by the wrist and I stood and followed, because the other choice would have been to be dragged like a rope behind him with the determined way he moved.

We wove our way around the party and into the clubhouse. Music blasted through speakers, bodies moved together twirling with fast footwork. We went up a flight of stairs, then another, until he dragged me to a room down the hall.

I wasn't stupid. I knew he was taking me to his room. Just like I knew why. Men were so fucking infuriating and also so predictable. He said he didn't want me because I was his employee, but he also wouldn't let anyone else flirt with me? How fucked up was that? And why was I a puta for such behavior?

He closed and locked the door behind him then gave me a shove in the direction towards the bed. I fell onto my ass, my breathing speeding up.

I knew what he wanted.

I wanted it, too.

Even if he was a huge, possessive, machista asshole, I fucking wanted it. Because in that moment, none of his defects mattered. It didn't matter that he was my boss. That he'd fired me. That he'd barely spoken two words to me since we'd met. That he was acting like a jealous boyfriend when he literally had no right to do so.

All that mattered was the other things. The way he'd had someone paint my ma's house. The angry way he'd shoved a prospect's face into a wall for disrespecting me. The tender way his smirk kicked up when he thought my ideas were good. The way he lifted my chin and let me lose myself in his gaze.

The way he'd cleaned the blood off my hands and ensured I was protected and didn't cower back from the shadows and monsters that plagued me from the inside.

Even if he was silent in his demands, his eyes did the speaking for him. And I understood every fucking word.

His slow perusal of my body ignited my skin, settling every nerve and vein ablaze. Where his eyes tracked, licks of fire trailed after until I felt too hot, too uncomfortable. I shifted, letting myself fall slowly back against his mattress. My brows kicked up, a smirk touched my lips. A challenge and a dare both.

If he thought I was going to fight him on this, to argue, to remind him that we were nothing but boss and employee, he had another thing coming. Did I think starting something was wrong? I did. Yet my stomach twisted up into knots when he was near. I felt safe in his presence, and I wanted to know—at least once—what it felt like to be taken care of by someone else instead of the other way around.

So, yeah. This was a terrible idea. But I knew what doing this meant. It wouldn't change anything, it wouldn't make him fall for me, and the next day when we were done, we'd go back to being boss and employee. Nothing more, and certainly nothing less.

Our eyes held, but my hands moved of their own volition, sliding across my body in a sensuous dance down my sides, over my breasts and lower still. Ink tore his gaze from mine to track my movements. He bit along his bottom lip.

The quiet wasn't unnerving. It only emboldened me. My fingers flicked at the button on my jeans and the zipper slid down, material parting to reveal the tight, black boxers I wore beneath.

He finally moved, stalking forward until his knees hit the bed. Every movement he made was confident, sure.

I liked that about him. I liked that there was no hesitation in this, when there had been before. I liked that he stared at me like I was something–someone–to be admired. Someone he couldn't take his eyes off of.

His fingers hooked into the waist of my jeans, and he yanked on the material, pulling them down the length of my legs. I helped him, kicking them and my boots off. There was no awkward moment. No stopping. Just heat pressing between us, rising as his body fell over mine. He held himself up by the hands and stared down at me.

"I'll ask this once." His voice vibrated all down my chest, tightening my core. "Do you want this?"

I cocked an eyebrow daringly. "You didn't seem too concerned about me wanting this when you dragged me up here in front of everybody."

"Xiomara." My name was a mere warning on his lips.

My breath hitched, and I reevaluated my answer, "I'm here, aren't I?"

"Hmm." He reached between me and the mattress to grasp my neck, holding me firm. I liked the roughness of his fingers digging into my skin. "If at any point you want me to stop–"

"I won't." I wanted this more than I wanted air. I wasn't sure when it happened, how it happened, but at one point between us the lines had blurred. I was drowning in life, in grief, in anger, and it was only him who could save me.

"But if you do–"

My hands wrapped around his waist and yanked him down so his body was flush against mine. The scrape of his jeans against my boxer-clad pussy nearly had me moaning. I rubbed myself against him, searching for friction against my clit. Little bursts of sensation flicked through me at the contact, but it wasn't nearly enough.

"Ink." I was breathless. "Fuck me. Now. Hard. I don't want to talk or think."

Take control, my eyes pleaded.

I wanted the promise of safety. I wanted the loss of control. I wanted the release of brutality. A fight for pleasure and pain. I wanted everything I knew Ink could give me and *more*. If only to feel. For once in my life.

He emitted a low growl before he pulled away from me. Something in his eyes darkened even deeper than the shadows in the room.

He didn't speak again as he grabbed me by the hips and flipped me face down against the mattress. His hands were rough and demanding as they yanked my lower half up until my knees were planted firmly on the mattress, ass in the air.

I buried my face into the covers, biting down on the material to avoid mewling like I really wanted to. My hands tightened into fists when Ink's fingers pulled at the black boxers, sliding them over the curve of my ass.

A draft of cold hit me as he shoved it down my thighs. His rough palms warmed me right up again as he squeezed and kneaded, touching me at his leisure. I sighed softly, nearly melting into the mattress right before a yelp came out of me when his hand cracked down against my skin.

The slap stung, and yet when he did it again on the other cheek, the brief bite of pain gave way to a different sensation that had me flooding, wet and eager. A groan of absolute pleasure rippled through me. I wiggled my ass, wanting more of that pain while rubbing my thighs together for much needed friction. But he didn't slap me again. At the slide of his stubbled cheek against my skin, I twisted my head at an uncomfortable angle to stare at him.

The kisses he trailed against me left warmth, and I could feel the soft scraping of his jawline against my light brown skin. Holding my hips tightly with his hand, Ink leaned forward, and I cried out as his tongue licked a stripe up my pussy.

"Fuck." My hands tightened even further, everything in me electrifying at the warm, wet touch.

"You like that?" His voice rumbled against me.

"Yes."

I liked it a lot, and I wanted more of it. More of him. Suddenly I was dripping, aching to be filled to the brim with his cock. I leaned back a fraction, my version of begging, even if I wouldn't say the words.

Because Ink understood me–perhaps more than anyone else–he chuckled, smacking my ass lightly enough to send a frisson of excitement throughout my body.

"My cock is too hard for foreplay," he growled.

"And I'm too wet to be bothered with it."

I liked foreplay–who didn't?–but we'd been dancing around one another for far too long already. I didn't want to wait any longer.

"Fuck me," I said. "Hard. As hard as you fucking can."

I heard the clink of his belt, the slide of a zipper. Everything inside me trembled with anticipation for what was to come. The shuffle of his jeans as he shoved them down. His hands on my hips as he yanked me backwards.

JADE HERNÁNDEZ

I counted down the seconds, waiting, holding my breath.

The tip of his cock pressed against my folds, hot, slick. I clenched around empty air, my body all but begging to hug him close.

With one hand digging into my hip, the other lashed out to grab me by the back of the neck. It was precisely the kind of roughness I needed to send my thoughts flying. He buried my face into the blankets. For a moment, I couldn't breathe. Fear gripped me the longer he kept me face down, so long that my lungs screamed, and yet the pleasure only *heightened* alongside the unknown danger of the moment.

He was suffocating me and it was only in the best of ways.

Digging into my neck, he yanked my head back up a fraction and I gulped a lungful of air, right before he shoved me face down onto the mattress once more and thrust into me from behind.

My scream was muffled as his thick cock stretched me to fullness. I gasped for breath, but he only pushed my face down harder right before he began to thrust.

Brutal snaps of his hips met mine. The wet noises of our joining echoing through the room. He grunted with every plunge inside, his cock splitting me open from behind, pushing in and out of my channel with the violent ease of someone who owned my body.

And maybe he did. At least for this moment in time. He owned me, and my body wept and begged for more, pulling him into my pussy, throbbing around him.

I grew lightheaded with lack of air, feeling my vision fade around the edges. I trembled and he yanked me up to breathe.

"Ink," I whispered. It was the only word I could make myself utter before he began his relentless assault on my body again. We were only half naked, and yet the heat that flowed between us was enough to scorch me down to my soul. His grunts became a soundtrack in my ears, and eventually I joined him in my cries.

He wasn't kind. He wasn't gentle. His palms slapped at my ass, the sting building an ache that almost sent me spiraling right then. My arms flailed, hands grasping at nothing. Ink just yanked me closer, pushing inside me so deep, I swore I could feel him in my fucking throat.

"You like this, huh?" His hand snaked beneath me to palm my breast. It was painful, the way he squeezed, but it sent every thought flying from my brain.

I rocked back against him. "Yesss..." He pinched my nipple, causing the word to come out in a hiss.

"Sí, Xiomara. *Tómalo todo.* Take my fucking cock. Take it all." he snapped his hips against mine, bowing over me. His every rough breath blew against my cheek, the weight of his body a suffocating comfort that I relished in as my body pulled taut.

"Yes, yes, give it to me. *Dámelo.*" My pleas spurred him on, faster, harder. Every vicious thrust sent a zing through my clit. He hadn't touched me there, and yet his hips pressed my own onto the bed, creating a contrasting friction between his violence and the softness of the covers. It kept me on the edge of an orgasm, something within my grasp only to be yanked away each time.

"I want to fill you with my cum," Ink growled, and the words sounded like a fucking threat. The danger of that implication made a thrill shoot through me. Like we were playing a game of chance. It shouldn't have turned me on as much as it did, but...

"Sí," I begged. "Yes. Yes. Yes!"

I wasn't sure what I was begging for in that moment, if I was pleading for my release or pleading for him to cum inside me. I was aware of the hot pulse of his cock and the lack of protection between us. It was irresponsible, and I couldn't bring myself to give a single fuck when he was pushing me to the edge of where I wanted to be.

My orgasm crested and I chased the sensation. My hips slammed back against his in desperate wanting.

"Oh, fuck, Xiomara..."

The guttural way he said my name was what finally sent me over the edge. I spiraled, free-falling through a void without a parachute. I cried out, screaming into the blanket as he continued his assault.

It was perfect.

It was vicious.

It was brutal.

And it was safe.

The warmth of his cum filled my insides. His cock swelled just before his release claimed him, and he bowed over me, thrusting in snapping inelegance against my body as he chased his own release. I squeezed tightly around him, causing a curse to slip from his lips.

He fell against my back a fraction of a second before hoisting himself up. The loss of his touch was like being flayed open. My breaths came out harshly, but I didn't move.

His fingers hooked back into the waist of my boxers and he yanked them up. The dark material caught the sliding warmth of his cum, pressing it back against my pussy.

Ink patted my ass, and there was affection in the gesture. I was sure of it.

"We're going to go back out to the party," he said in a harsh exhale. "And you're going to keep my cum inside you like a good girl."

I nearly whimpered at the words. But he wasn't done with me. He leaned over me again, his scraping jawline passing against my cheek.

"And while you're flirting with my club brothers, you'll do it with my fucking seed inside you."

It was probably the most he'd ever spoken to me. It was with a whispered hint of violence and anger. It was possessive when it had no right to be. But all my earlier irritation fled, replaced with a strange warmth that spread from my head down to my toes.

His seed was inside of me, and it felt like he'd branded me. It was ridiculous, irresponsible. I should have been pissed off that he hadn't used a condom, but the thrill of the risk outweighed any sense I should have had in my addled brain.

Fuck if that wasn't dangerous.

But fuck if I cared.

I pushed myself up on shaking arms and turned in time to see him zip his cock back into his pants. I'd barely gotten a glimpse of it, and my mouth watered, suddenly wanting more. But Ink wasn't staring at me. His jaw was hard, his veins twitching.

I wondered if this was the part where he began to regret what we'd done. If he wasn't already.

That didn't sting, though. It should have, but I was still riding the high of my own bliss that I let it roll off my shoulders.

I was a big fucking girl. I knew this was a one-time thing. And I wasn't going to regret this, just like I wasn't going to let what had transpired here come between my relationship with Ink.

He was my boss. That was it.

Even if a part of me wanted something more.

Chapter Eleven
Ink

I DIPPED MY COCK into an employee. Even worse, I'd spent myself inside her like a goddamn teen. But did I care about all that? No. Xiomara Nava made me lose my good sense in the best possible fucking way.

I knew why that was. I knew why I couldn't get her out of my head ever since I'd met her. It was the same reason she invaded my every fucking thought since the moment I'd walked into my own damn shop to see her holding a bat, covered in blood like some type of avenging goddess with dead men at her feet.

Los Diablos lived a life of fast, dangerous debauchery. We couldn't afford to second guess ourselves. When we saw something we wanted, we fucking took it. We stole it. No questions asked.

I didn't have the right to cum inside her, but the moment she stripped herself bare for me and begged me to fuck her hard and fast, I knew she was meant to be mine. I no longer gave a fuck that she was an employee and that I was breaking my own frigid rules by getting involved with her.

I wanted Xiomara, and I'd have her. So I'd marked her. If that made me a neanderthal, so be it. But my cum had dripped from her pretty little cunt, which made her mine. And when we walked out of the clubhouse and she went and flirted with my club brothers like I knew she would, I only kept my anger in check because I knew her pussy was dripping wet with a piece of me.

The next day at work, she barely spoke to me. I could tell she'd erected a wall between us, even after I'd fucked her into my mattress. She'd gone back to giving me the cold shoulder, and I hadn't spoken to her either.

The day started off slow, but eventually customers filed in to create appointments. I was sanitizing the back when I first heard it.

Xiomara's laughter.

The sound was like a fucking punch to the gut, something that immediately irritated me when it was followed by a man's laughter. I let out a curse that had Fer side-eyeing me from her station. I ignored her and stormed to the front only to find some dickhead with his palms against *my* desk leaning in *my* woman's direction.

The smile he gave her was flirtatious, and the one she gave him back was equally so.

As if sensing my presence behind her, she turned, and her smile dropped. "Ink," she greeted in a droll tone. As if I hadn't made her scream my fucking name the day before. As if she hadn't orgasmed all over me. As if she hadn't begged "*Dámelo*" as I speared her with my cock or marked her with my seed.

My glare went to the man there. He was still staring at Xiomara.

As if he had a fucking chance.

"What do you want?" My barked question finally had his attention turning to me. He wasn't someone I'd ever tatted before, but there were always referrals coming through my shop doors. Friends of people I'd worked on in the past.

"I'm here to set an appointment."

My brows kicked up. "Really? Because it looks like you're flirting with my woman."

He seemed to visibly pale at my words, eyes darting down to my cut. He knew what the fucking patch meant. He knew the weight my fucking club had.

Which meant he knew I was capable of ripping his guts out through his asshole.

"Get the fuck out of my shop."

He turned tail and ran like a little fucking bitch. When he was gone, I faced Xiomara's glare head-on.

"What the hell?" she demanded. "You have no right. You're my boss, not my keeper."

It seemed my woman needed a fucking reminder about who owned her ass.

I reached for her wrist and yanked her towards me. "Shut the fuck up," I barked when she opened her mouth to argue.

She clamped her mouth closed again, huffing a breath. I pulled her towards the back area. Fer eyed us with a small smirk, but I didn't have time for her bullshit.

"Get out," I said. "And lock the shop up behind you."

She cackled and ignored Xiomara, even as my woman threw her a pleading look. It wasn't until I heard Fer leave the shop and twist the lock behind her that I shoved Xiomara down onto the leather tattoo chair.

"What the fuck are you doing, Ink?"

I climbed over her, straddling her hips and pinning her down.

"Take off your fucking shirt."

Her cheeks colored at my command, but she tilted her chin up in an act of defiance. "No," she said firmly.

"If you don't, I'll rip it off of you."

"Ink, you're my boss. What the fuck do you think you're doing? Why are you acting like you own me?" There was the slightest tremble of her voice, and as I stared into her eyes, I could read her emotions clearly.

She was afraid.

Afraid of my answer, and the changes it would bring between us, yet she wanted me. Almost as much as I wanted her.

I leaned down so the tips of our noses touched. "I branded you with my cum," I reminded her. Her cheeks heated. "You're mine, Xiomara. I don't give a fuck that you're my employee. *Eres mía.* And I'm going to remind you of that fact. Now take off your fucking shirt."

Her breath hitched and her pupils flared. She liked this. She liked me rough and mean and dominating. "What are you going to do?"

"I'm not going to ask you a third time, nena."

Her trembling fingers went to do my bidding. I liked that about her. She had a bite to her, but she was quick to obey her man. She liked the direction. Liked to be controlled, to be taken care of.

I watched as the shirt came off from over her shoulders, leaving her bare in nothing but a lacy black bra that pushed her breasts up for my admiration.

Perfect.

I leaned down, pressing a kiss over one of her curves.

She sighed softly, leaning into my touch like she was starved for it.

She could argue as much as she wanted, but she and I both knew that she wanted this.

"I thought I'd made myself clear." I reached off to a side table, gripping a rag with alcohol. I brought it down to her breast, swiping the area I'd claimed. "You're mine, Xiomara."

She wiggled beneath me. "What do you mean, yours?"

I slapped a pair of latex gloves on. "Eres mi Vieja," I said.

Her eyes widened at the declaration, and she mouthed the words back to me in shock.

I grabbed and prepped my tattoo gun and turned it on, dipping it in black ink before I brought it towards her skin.

"Wait–" Her voice trembled. "We haven't even *kissed* yet and you're calling me your Old Lady."

"I don't need to fucking kiss you to know I'm claiming you. Now don't fucking move." The buzz of the gun filled the room.

Xiomara didn't move.

I knew she wouldn't. And yet it felt good to see she was as on board with this as I was.

The gun pressed against her skin, and she winced a moment before sighing deep, almost leaning into the pain of the needles. I worked carefully, not even needing a stencil as I looped swirls and letters against her flesh. My gaze occasionally flicked up to find her staring at me, her painted little mouth dropped open as she breathed through her arousal.

With a smirk, I pressed harder onto her, with the hardness of my cock and the gun. Her response was immediate. She thrust up into me and I had the foresight to yank the gun away before the jerking of her body fucked up my neat scrawl.

I frowned down at her, even as jagged shards of pleasure shot through my chest at her inhibitions. "Don't move," I ordered.

Her answering moan was all too bratty. Setting aside the gun momentarily, I leaned over her, palming her pussy through her jeans in a single, rough touch. She exhaled sharply, nostrils flaring, and the fire in her answering glare had my dick jerking within the confines of my jeans.

"If you move, I'll have to punish you."

Her breath caught and it was followed by a whimpering sound that had me fighting back my own groan. *Fuck.*

"Be a good girl like I know you can be and don't fucking move." I waited patiently to see what she'd do. Instead of nodding, her lush mouth dropped open.

"Okay," she agreed.

I smirked. While that single word was her submission, there was a daring flare in her eyes that was begging for the promise of a bruising touch and the brutal edge of my demands. And beneath all of that, there were more vulnerable layers piled on but that desperate urge and need for release rose to the top.

I wouldn't leave her wanting.

With slow precision, my fingers undid the button of her jeans and slid the zipper down. The material parted to reveal her boxers. I played with the edge of the elastic, pulling it back and letting go so it slapped against her smooth skin.

"This is going to be a bit of a challenge," I whispered, eyes flicking back up to meet hers. "I've never fucked someone and given them a tattoo at the same time."

Her breath hitched.

I smirked.

"You'll have to sit very, very still for me." I yanked the latex glove off one hand with my teeth, letting it fall away to the side. "I wouldn't want to ruin your pretty skin."

My fingers slipped within the confines of her boxers, tracing over the soaking slit of her pussy. Finding her wet and ready made me want to dive face first into her and suck her off until she was screaming my name.

Tracing the wetness of her folds, I slid a single finger up against her sweet little clit, smearing it with her own juices.

She gave the slightest of jerks against the touch, subtle enough that I kept going, tracing small circles against her nub with my calloused fingers. When she whimpered, I slid back to her slit, teasing her lower lips with two fingers.

I played just enough to satisfy an itch, but kept her on a precipice that had her mouth singing for me. The crescendo of her cries echoed around us, yet she kept herself as still as she could.

I smirked as she trembled from the effort, rewarding her by slipping a finger into her channel.

"Fuck. *Ink—*"

I reached for the gun once again and hovered over her, bringing it down against her breast.

"Don't move," I reminded her right before I turned it on and began my brand all over again.

Her light brown skin darkened with my ink while my fingers stretched inside her. Another one slid inside, scissoring several times. She gushed against me, juices sliding down my fingers and against my wrist.

"Ink—" Her breath stuttered out of her.

I paused long enough to look up and see her biting down hard against her bottom lip. Hard enough to draw blood.

With deliberate slowness, I pulled the gun away and slipped my fingers from her pussy, bringing them up to her mouth. They caressed her bottom lip, a tender gesture I never knew I was capable of making before.

She had no fucking idea just how bright she was. Like the sun, and I was powerless to the pull of her orbit.

"Taste how wet you are for me, baby."

She released the brutal hold on her lip, dark eyes hooded as she dropped that mouth I desperately wanted to fuck open. I shoved my fingers inside and she lapped up her own essence like it was candy.

I jerked my hips against her in a poor imitation of what I wanted to do to her.

"Such a good fucking girl, aren't you?" I pulled my fingers from her mouth and she released them with a pop. They immediately went back into her boxers and to her pussy.

I wasn't slow or tender this time. I shoved my way inside with a force that made her cry out and jerk in surprise.

"Hmm," I hummed. "Que rica estás. I can't wait to fuck you again."

Once again, the gun found itself into my hand, the buzzing drowning out her cries of pleasure and pain as the needle touched her skin. I resumed digging it into her flesh, swooping and whirling, my movements purposefully slow as I divided my attention between the tattoo and her weeping pussy.

"Sí, mójame. Get me so fucking wet, baby."

Her pussy drenched around my moving fingers, soaking down to my palms with every thrust in and out.

"Ink. I–I can't–" Her hips canted up a fraction.

The needles dug deeper into her skin, darkening her even further. I curved my fingers inside at the same time, relishing in the sound of her cries.

"You're trying so hard to keep still aren't you, baby?"

I usually didn't like to speak when I fucked. There never was a reason when I usually dipped my dick into club putas. They weren't with me for the conversation, and I wasn't either.

She was different.

She needed this. From the way her insides squeezed me like she could choke the life out of my fingers, strangle my pulse, swallow me fucking whole, I knew she *loved* my words.

Every dirty fucking bit of them.

"Fuck, baby." I let out a low hiss when her walls fluttered around me. She was close. I could feel it.

But so was I.

"No. Don't you dare fucking cum, Xiomara."

She whimpered in response.

I slowed my thrusting, sweeping her wetness out and against her clit. A final test. It burned against my fingers as I circled it.

"Don't cum," I ordered.

"Ink—"

"Don't." I flicked her clit. Hard. She gasped, the sound drowned out by the buzz as I neared the end of the tattoo.

"Mírate nada más. Tan mojada, tan caliente. So wet and hot for my cock. You like pain with your pleasure, baby? You want to be fucking spanked? Choked?"

She let out a low hiss and a moan. "Yessss..."

"Te lo voy a dar," I promised. "Te lo daré todo."

She was right there on the crest of her orgasm. I could feel it. Sense it.

I wanted it but not yet.

My hands pulled from her boxers and she cried out a protest but I ignored it. Wet fingers met her neck, pinning her down as gently as I could manage.

"Do you know why I am going to give you everything?"

Her eyes begged me to answer the question quickly, but I simply smirked.

Painting her flesh was such a fucking turn on. Marking her permanently to remind her who owned her now–not just in body but soul as well. Blood seeped through the ink and when I finished the last looping letter, I set the gun aside to swipe and disinfect her skin one-handed.

Seeing the product of my obsession had my heart beating a rhythm that matched the screaming pulsations of my rock-hard cock. I smiled down at Xiomara and the new tattoo I'd given her, marked forever on her flesh for everyone to see.

Property of Ink.

Chapter Twelve
Xiomara

P<small>ROPERTY OF</small> I<small>NK</small> in cursive, swirling letters glared at me from the top of my breast. The liberties he took with my own body should have infuriated me, and yet I fought hard not to squirm beneath him because I was so fucking turned on. So close to falling into that blissful release that would leave me mind-numbingly boneless.

The pain of the tattoo gun piercing my flesh had caused desire to flow freely through me. Pairing that with the curl and thrusting of his fingers?

My body was on fire. Every piece of me felt electrified, shock waves threatening to blast through every fucking crevice. It was *right* there, the sensation of wanting to implode, yet so far away at the same time.

It made me furious.

And yet truth be told, being claimed? I wanted it. I wanted to belong to someone like him. Someone who had an entire club at his back. Someone demanding. Possessive. Someone who would protect and care about me. I didn't care that he probably did illegal shit. I didn't care that he marked me without permission, because I'd given him my fucking heart and soul from the moment he'd gone to my house without even knowing it.

Even if we hadn't kissed.

As soon as he tossed the now silent tattoo gun off to the side and stared down at his own handiwork, a sigh left me. Our eyes caught, flared. We reached for one another, our mouths colliding for the first time ever in a sudden vicious fight for dominance. I yielded to him, tongues tangling, breaths mingling. Our bodies plastered together and I hissed against his mouth at the sting I felt against my breast.

Yet he wasn't careful. If anything, my pain spurred him on and only made me wetter. He grasped at my newly tattooed breast in his hand, squeezing the spot he'd marked as his own.

Property of Ink.

I was his now. I belonged to him. His Vieja, his Old Lady. I was a MC wife, and I'd be protected by him and the club. That sense of security, that sense of fucking promise, was something I'd always needed and wanted.

And I finally had it.

I moaned, rubbing my lower half against him.

"Fuck me," I pleaded, tearing my mouth away from his. "Fuck me right here."

He tore at my jeans, slipping me out of my clothes. He stripped himself until he was naked in front of me. My breath caught, eyes tracing the lines of dark ink that circled his entire body. They curved across his muscles and over his veins, images of skulls and devils, of Catrinas and flor de cempazuchitl, of big breasted women and Mayan imagery.

He was a god.

I swore I whimpered right then, causing him to chuckle as he laid himself over me. Just like last time, he entered me in a single thrust. I was still sore from him yesterday, but the pain was entirely too pleasant and wanted. I groaned as his bare cock slid in and out of me.

I didn't give a fuck that he was bare. I'd take another pill, get a prescription, do anything if it meant I got to feel every pulsing, thick inch.

My hips rose to meet his and soon, he was thrusting hard, wrapping his hand across my throat to keep me pinned to the chair. I gasped for breath once again, digging my fingers into his chest. He leaned down as I marked him with the crescents of my nails, and he took my mouth in his.

The kiss was everything. When he broke away to trail his tongue down my neck, only to scrape his stubble across my tattooed breast, I felt myself falling into a steadfast orgasm.

I whirled and cried out, falling, falling. I was sure I was screaming his name.

He grunted in my ear, cumming inside me like he'd done yesterday.

That marking was intimate in a way that made me tremble.

When we came down from our bliss, Ink wrapped me in his arms and held me close. It was different from yesterday. A display of affection I craved as he held me close, pushing strands of my hair aside.

"Did I hurt you?" he whispered.

"Only in the best way."

"Hmm." His calloused fingers slid against the edge of my tattoo, not touching or tracing, but staring down at it with a bit of wonder.

Maybe he thought I was going to stop him.

Would he have listened if I had asked him to? It didn't matter, because I wouldn't have.

"In case it wasn't clear," he began, "you're mine, Xiomara."

"And you're mine, too?" I hadn't meant for it to come out as a question. But it did. I wasn't a part of the MC life–though now I was. I knew how dynamics worked. The club putas were there to suck off the guys, whether they were taken or not. I wasn't sure it mattered. Maybe I was asking him if he was going to be loyal to me. But I knew I had to outright say it. My fingers traced the face of a Catrina on his pec. "My dad walked out on us," I whispered. I hated talking about the bastard but if I did then maybe he would've understood my fears. "He went to the U.S.A., sent money a few times, and then disappeared."

Ink frowned. "He dead?"

I huffed a breath. "Social media shows him happy with his new family over there. Left me, my siblings, and my ma to fend for ourselves. After he made her quit work to be a housewife, he abandoned her with no money. We all had to fight to support each other and help ma pay the bills."

"Hmm." His fingers brushed aside my hair. "I won't do that to you."

"I didn't think my dad would do that to me either."

I could sense his irritation. "I'm not a fucking deadbeat," he snarled. "I said you're mine, and that's a fucking promise. You're my Vieja now, and I'm going to take care of you. You want to work? Fine, work, do whatever the fuck you want with your time, but know that I am going to be behind you, beside you, wherever the fuck you want me." He grasped my chin tightly, tilting my head up to press a firm kiss to my lips. "Why the fuck would I want anyone else when I've got you?"

My heart melted at those words. I wasn't one to fall for prose so easily, and yet he didn't wax poetic. He didn't say it like some smooth-talking jackass.

When he said those words, I believed them.

"I believe you," I said, fingers threading through his short hair. I grasped tightly, yanking his head back. "But if you fuck around on me with a club puta, I will shoot them in the head and then cut off your fucking dick."

The words had his dick hardening between us. "Hmm." He pressed a kiss to my jawline. "I like you possessive and violent."

And he may not have realized it, but those words were better than any love declaration he could ever make.

Chapter Thirteen
Xiomara

Weeks passed by and the group of MC brothers that had surrounded the shop for protection slowly trickled down to nothing but a few prospects. They'd declared things relatively safe, though I wasn't worried. Ink was more worried than me, but I told him I could take care of myself.

To that, he'd just pinched my chin between his thumb and forefinger and glared down at me. "I swore to take care of you, and I'm going to."

He didn't know how those words affected me. In every possible way.

Ink had flaunted me around the clubhouse as his Vieja almost immediately. True to Ink fashion, he'd just stalked behind me, making me wear a shirt with low cleavage to show off the bright handiwork on my skin.

I hadn't minded the gesture or the almost feral way he glared at his own brothers for hugging me in congratulations. It had resulted in my ass getting reddened from how hard he'd slapped it and a sore pussy from how brutally he'd thrusted in me.

While his friends and family had immediately accepted me into their fold, my ma was reluctant to trust him. I knew—even if she didn't want me to–that she was coming around. Ink was going above and beyond trying to impress her.

She didn't like his domineering ways, but I could see the etched relief on her features every time he showed up at our house to fix something that had been broken for years and we couldn't afford to fix. The toilet, the leaky ceiling, the piece of shit car. He'd even made the prospects clean the yard and plant new flowers, considering work had made her neglect her plant babies.

My siblings had all but accepted him, calling him cuñado in a show of affection.

I think my ma was just mad he gave me a tattoo. Or maybe she was worried I'd get hurt like she had. But if there was something I knew with absolute clarity it was that Ink was nothing like my dad, and he would never, ever hurt me.

"I'm heading out," Ink said, slapping my ass as he passed by me. I yelped and shot him a fake look of annoyance. "Loco called a meeting. Prospect's outside to watch you."

"I don't need a babysitter," I reminded him, just like I'd been reminding him for days now. He didn't discuss club business with me, not that I cared, but he had told me that things were quiet.

I lived for the quiet, while it made him nervous.

"You'll do what I say." Ink pierced me with a glare.

I liked when he got bossy. When he took control, even outside of sex. Especially in moments like these. It was a relief knowing he cared so much, that he was willing to protect me in ways no one else had.

"Fine." I huffed out a breath. "Should I wait for you?"

He shook his head. "Church might run late tonight. Lock up and the prospect will take you home."

My own painted brows kicked up. "Really? On the back of his bike? I'll be plastered all over his body, you know..."

He let out a low growl and would have reached for me by the neck if the desk wasn't between us. "I'm going to spank that ass later."

"I look forward to it."

He shot me one of his rare smiles before he walked out of the shop. From outside on the street, I could make out the prospect standing there. Ink stopped to speak with him for a moment, likely to threaten his life if he tried anything with me, before he left.

I hurried through the motions of closing time, cleaning meticulously every nook and cranny. It didn't matter that I was with Ink now. He was still my boss, and I still had a job to do. He wouldn't let me off the hook just because we were fucking. So I suffered through the stench of lemon cleaner and when I finally finished, let out a breath of relief.

After packing up my bag and switching off the light, I walked outside to meet the prospect.

He inhaled a drag of his cigarette, nodding at me. "Ready to go?"

"Yup."

He tossed the cigarette to the ground and used his heel to stomp on it. "Right, let's–"

He never got the rest of his sentence out, because a bullet shot straight through his body.

The prospect jerked, in shock, pain, or both. He took a step, clutching at his chest just as a bright spot of red bloomed against his shirt.

The shock kept me standing where I was, staring at him with my mouth gaped open. Our eyes met and he murmured one word right before a second bullet hit between his eyes. Blood and brain matter splattered against me right before he fell.

A third shot rang out, this one zinging near my feet. It was what finally sprang me into motion. I dropped everything, turned, and did what the prospect had asked me to do.

I fucking ran.

I didn't get very far. Even as I zigzagged across the street, trying to hide beneath the cover of shadows. A searing pain hit me in the shoulder and I went tumbling down on the ground.

I let out a guttural cry that resounded through the night. But even as I screamed, I knew no one would come. When people heard bullets, they hid. When people heard a woman cry out, they looked the other way.

I got to my feet, darkness clouding over me as an all-too familiar rage settled into the recesses of my bones.

I tried to take a step, but the cocking of a gun stopped me.

I swallowed and turned where I stood, meeting crisp blue eyes, bright like chips of ice.

And I knew then, that there would be no escaping this time.

Chapter Fourteen
Ink

Shooting the shit with my brothers was something present in every meeting, depending on the severity of things. Tonight, things were tense, but not so tense that jokes weren't cracked in between the silences.

Loco sat at the head of the table, staring pointedly down into his whiskey glass, a pensive look on his face.

It gave everyone pause.

"Those hijos de puta are up to something," he said finally, tapping his fingers against the table. "They've been too fucking quiet."

"Three of their men have been buried," Miguel, the VP of the club, tried to reason in that calm demeanor that always contrasted Loco's. "Maybe they're trying to find them."

Loco shook his head. "Nah. Those bastardos know they're dead and don't give a fuck. They're plotting something. We need to reach out to some of our contacts, see where they could be staying. Flush them out."

"How long will that take?" I asked, arms crossed tightly against my chest. Every eye turned to me. I wasn't one of the officers, but we all had equal say at the table.

"It takes however long it fucking takes," Loco said, eyeing me steadily.

"Too fucking long," I growled. "We should move faster."

"Do you think they'll go after your Vieja?" Miguel asked. His tone was much more pleasant than Loco's. The levelheaded VP was always one to think first, instead of act. In that way he differed from Loco's hotheadedness.

"I don't know, but I don't want to take that chance."

"If you're so worried about your woman, why don't you lock her up in your house? Get her barefoot and pregnant in the kitchen cooking for you."

A flare of irritation swept through me at Loco's nonchalant words. It showed how little he knew about my Vieja. She didn't want kids yet, and neither did I. Sure, we played it close to the chest with our lack of protection every time we fucked, but she was on the pill.

Loco smirked before taking a swig of his drink and slamming the glass back down on the table.

"Lighten the fuck up. She beat three grown ass men with a bat and came out with little damage. She can hold her fucking own."

"Yeah, but she shouldn't have to. Club shit isn't supposed to touch our families."

But it somehow always did.

Loco was about to say something, but was interrupted when his phone rang. Usually, phones weren't allowed in on church meetings, but as Loco was the prez, he could do whatever the fuck he wanted with little consequences. But he also only kept it on for emergencies, and he most certainly didn't answer if it wasn't one.

But he did answer, pressing it to his ear.

He listened to whoever was on the other end of the line and let out a curse. I knew immediately when his eyes landed on me that something was wrong.

And that something had to do with Xiomara.

He hung up and stood. "We have to fucking roll out." His eyes never once left mine.

I felt my heart trip through my chest. I didn't want to think the worst, and yet I couldn't stop the errant turn my thoughts took. The fear that sliced through my chest. A promise I made, broken, the pieces of it crumbling inside me like broken glass.

"What happened?"

"Shots fired at Devil's Ink," Loco explained. "The prospect's dead and your Vieja..."

He didn't get the rest of his sentence out. I was already moving, seeing red, something vicious awoken inside me as I rushed out to my bike and started it up.

My Vieja was fucking gone.

And whoever had taken her would fucking pay.

Chapter Fifteen
Xiomara

My legs kicked out, colliding with bodies that grappled with my struggling form. I grunted and screamed, even though logically I knew nobody was coming for me. The sounds tore out of me, wild and afraid, even when I didn't want them to.

I was already aching and in pain, but it didn't matter to my captors.

"Calm that bitch down."

I screamed as a fist collided against my cheek. I swore I saw stars and a crushing agony spreading through the entire left side of my face rendered me immobile almost immediately. I stopped fighting, the pain pushing out the cloud of rage momentarily.

My captors unceremoniously tossed me to the ground, causing the breath to whoosh from my lungs. I groaned in pain, rolling to my side to glare at the men.

There were four of them, and they all had guns.

Only one of them sported it, though. The others bulged through their shirts, the outline obvious.

The men had brought me to a warehouse of some sort. The fact that they hadn't blindfolded me was worrisome. It let me know that they didn't plan on letting me leave here alive.

But I'd fought like hell. Even with my shoulder screaming from the bullet lodged there, I'd fought.

And in this moment, I despaired as they crowded near me, discussing my future.

"Careful with the goods," one of them said. "Boss man wants the product intact."

When he said product, I knew he meant me.

My heart sunk to the bottom of my stomach.

"Are we allowed to have a go at her?" another asked, his eyes straying in my direction.

I glared right back, refusing to cower.

It'd be a cold day in hell when I let men like this intimidate me, let alone fucking touch me.

"No."

"But–"

"No," the obvious ringleader of the group repeated more firmly. "We wait for directions. Okay?"

"Fine." And like a petulant child, his leg kicked out, colliding with my body and making me wheeze.

"Fuck, did you not hear what I just said?"

I was going to make them pay. I was going to fucking kill them. But I needed to steal one of their guns first. Maybe I could lure one closer somehow. Take it from him. Shoot him in the head. Or use one as a hostage.

Would I get very far considering the pain I was in? I had no idea. But I knew I had to try.

"You boys are pathetic," I spat out at them. It drew their attention to me, all of them clenching their jaws in irritation. "Four men to take down one girl?" I laughed. "Bitches. You afraid of a little woman with a baseball bat? Is that why you had to ambush me with guns? Didn't want to end up like your bitch ass friends buried deep in the dirt?"

"Shut the fuck up, cunt." One of them slipped closer and I pretended to cower, sliding away from him but angling my body just so, preparing myself for anything. When he was close enough, I struck.

Because he'd expected me to cower, he didn't see me coming. He only felt when I yanked the gun from within the belt of his pants and aimed it at his face. A single flick of my fingers to take the safety off and I was shooting.

The low angle in which I shot at him ensured I didn't get him between the eyes, but the bullet did shoot his big ass nose, blowing the thing clean off.

He screamed and jerked backwards, his cries of agony and the gunshot distracting the others. Too late, they scrambled for their own weapons.

Too fucking late. I shot one in the chest and he went down, his own gun falling from his grasp and going off. The bullet whizzed somewhere, but I was already far too gone in my rage. I shot my targets, the blackness closing in. The piercing pain of a bullet prevented me from being dragged under. I tried not to double over, but getting hit with a bullet once again sent one of my shots far too wide. I missed the bastard by a hair's breadth, allowing him to advance on me.

He'd lost his own gun in the melee and took advantage of my distraction by body checking me. I cried out as I fell backwards, gravity making the gun slip from my hand.

The man landed on top of me, my head cracking against the ground. His fingers wrapped around my throat and squeezed.

Black spots danced behind my vision.

JADE HERNÁNDEZ

Fuck no. I didn't want to die here today.

Using my nails, I gouged through his fucking eyes like we were taught. He cried out and jerked away from me and my fist struck, hitting him in the jugular.

He choked and I heaved up with all my might, shoving him off me. I scrambled away from him, my body shaking and yet determined. He hauled on my pant legs, trying to pull me back towards him, but I was faster. My fingers closed around a gun and I whirled–

A shot rang out and he slumped forward. Nothing but a cadaver oozing blood from his chest.

But I hadn't...

"Xiomara!"

I looked over the dead man's shoulder and found Ink, gun in hand, rushing in my direction.

And the sight of him, so close, so fucking close, made me feel one thing. My lips curled into a smile as he dropped to his knees beside me, shoving the body away. He pulled me into his arms.

"You're safe," he whispered. "You're safe now, Xio. Te tengo. You're safe."

And as my eyes closed into a blissful sleep, I felt it down to my bones.

Chapter Sixteen
Xiomara

A few months later...

My fist struck out, punching Ink in the arm.

He jerked back in surprise, wincing before he glared down at me. "The fuck, Vieja?"

"Don't you Vieja me, cabrón!"

Though the nickname did always make me melt, I was not having it right then.

It started weeks ago. He'd started acting super cagey. Dodging me when I was around, refusing to take off his shirt when we fucked. I knew there was only one explanation.

He was stepping out on me with one of the club putas.

"Who?" I demanded.

His brows furrowed. "Who what, wild woman?"

"Was it Yasmín?" I demanded.

That one had tried sinking her claws into Ink right in front of my very own eyes. Always draping herself over him like she fucking owned him, like she was his Vieja when I was the one with his name tattooed across my breast. I'd gotten into fisticuffs with her so often that the club brothers had started placing bets any time we were in the same room.

I always won.

JADE HERNÁNDEZ

Of course.

If I could beat three men to death with a bat and kill three with a gun in a warehouse, with a bullet in my shoulder, bruised ribs, and a broken toe, I could fucking end her. Fuck around and find out.

"What about Yasmín?"

I punched him again. My rage rose to an astronomical scale. I was sure I was shouting, drawing clubhouse eyes in our direction. I didn't give a fuck. Somewhere behind us, I was sure I heard my ma whispering a prayer for patience.

"Stop pretending to be innocent. You're fucking her, aren't you?" I hit him again, letting my rage fly. "Why else don't you take your fucking shirt off, huh? You hiding hickeys under there, pendejo?"

I sent my fist flying, only Ink caught it that time. I tried to yank myself from his hold, but he held firm.

"Benny Juárez, if you know what's good for you, you'll let me go this instant."

"Better do as she says, *Benny*," Fer teased from somewhere behind us.

Loco cackled.

Ever since I'd found out Ink's real name—Benito Juárez—I'd taken to calling him Benny. It wasn't every day I found myself fucking the founder of the motherland.

It was a running joke that had become popular among the club brothers. It wasn't my fault he was named after the first president of Mexico. And maybe I laid the teasing on a little thick just so he'd spank me a little harder each time.

So the fuck what?

But I wasn't in a teasing mood right then.

If anything, I felt murderous.

"Christ, Vieja. Can you shut the fuck up?" Ink's hands tightened on my wrist.

I stood there dumbfounded. "You did not just say that to me…"

"I don't have hickeys," he said with an infuriating amount of patience.

"Then what the fuck—"

He sighed and stepped away from me. "This was supposed to be a fucking surprise, but of course, you had to go and ruin it."

I watched as he yanked the collar of his t-shirt down, revealing his left pec.

And the fresh ink that lay there.

My eyes watered immediately at the sight of it, but I kept the tears at bay.

"You didn't."

"I did."

I could feel other club members closing in on us to see what the fuss was about. Some of his brothers laughed and teased, but I barely heard their voices. I was too busy looking at him. More specifically, at the ink swooping against his skin.

"You're pussy whipped," Loco called out.

"Fuck you," Ink called back. Then he glared at me. "I am going to spank your ass so fucking hard for this shit you just pulled."

I smiled through the tears that started to fall. "Do your worst."

He knew I loved it when he got rough. But I loved this more. The evidence that he was as enamored with me as I was with him. Because that tattoo on his body?

It was better than any gift I'd ever received.

Swirling letters that matched my own.
Property of Xiomara.

The End

Acknowledgements

I DON'T REALLY KNOW how to start this except with a massive THANK YOU. I mean, that's what this section is for, right? (Ha, ha!) But in all seriousness, this series wouldn't have come to life without the help and encouragement of several people. Thank you to my group of author friends in The Latin Book Nook who helped me get out of my head and write a book set in Mexico. It may not seem like it, but I debated HEAVILY on the setting of this story and decided to stay true to my original plan and set it in the state I currently live in. So thanks to everyone who convinced me to stay true to myself and this story. Big thanks to Sue, Tatiana, and Jess for reading my mess and helping me find last minute errors. Your help is appreciated, essential, and your comments made me very excited. Thank you Lisa for all that you do for my unedited draft. Thanks to my Street Team, for dealing with my bullshit and the constant teasers I throw your way. Thanks to the Latinx Romance book babes on IG and TikTok for wanting a Latino Motorcycle Club and for hyping this series up once you found out I was writing one. You guys are the best community an author could ask for and I appreciate you each and every day!

Made in the USA
Monee, IL
20 August 2025

23817641R00090